LURES

LURES

[signed: Steven Ross Smith]

FICTIONS BY STEVEN ROSS SMITH

March 2000
at Aden Bowman

THE MERCURY PRESS

The publisher gratefully acknowledges the financial assistance of the Canada Council for the Arts and the Ontario Arts Council.

Cover design by Gordon Robertson
Cover photograph by P. Elaine Sharpe
Edited by Beverley Daurio
Composition and page design by Task

Printed and bound in Canada by Metropole Litho
Printed on acid-free paper
First Edition
1 2 3 4 5 01 00 99 98 97

Canadian Cataloguing in Publication

Smith, Steven
Lures
ISBN 1-55128-051-8
I. Title
PS8587.M59L87 1997   813'.54   C97-932049-6
PR9199.3.S64L87 1997

Represented in Canada by the Literary Press Group
Distributed in Canada by General Distribution Services

The Mercury Press
2569 Dundas Street West
Toronto, Ontario
CANADA M6U 1X7

Dedicated to my mother

Ruth Marion (McDonald) Smith

who showed me the pliancy of words.

ACKNOWLEDGEMENTS

I wish to acknowledge several people, organizations, and situations, without which this book would not have been written.

Rosemary Nixon is a fine fiction writer and remarkable editor, and her blunt and positive feedback over several years kept throwing me back into many of these stories to re-visit crude versions with a sharper pencil. The encouragement of my mate, fiction writer J. Jill Robinson, was unwavering, and her editorial eye caught the glare in some of these fictions and aimed me toward beneficial polishings. Early encouragement and comment was offered by Laureen Marchand, Gerry Shikatani, and Paul Wilson. Thank you to Patricia Gonzalez for her knowledge of Colombia. And a nod to Michael Dean, who first told me that I ought to write fiction.

I was granted financial support, that bought time to write and tune this manuscript, by three indispensable agencies— Saskatchewan Arts Board, Canada Council for the Arts, and the Ontario Arts Council Writers' Reserve Program.

I began writing these stories when serving as Writer-in-Residence in Weyburn, Saskatchewan in 1987, in a residency supported by the Saskatchewan Writers Guild, Weyburn Public Library, and SaskLotteries. I completed the manuscript during a term in 1996-97 as Writer-in-Residence at the Saskatoon Public Library, a residency supported by SaskLotteries, Saskatchewan Arts Board, and Saskatoon Public Library.

I wish to express my gratitude to the Saskatchewan Writers Guild, for maintaining their Writers' and Artists' Colonies at Emma Lake and at St. Peter's Abbey, where I found the seclusion and concentration that allowed me to begin, develop, and complete many of these fictions.

I am grateful to Beverley Daurio for her faith in this work, and her judicial editorial hand. Finally, thanks to the painters of the works which inspired two of these pieces: Christine Lynn, for *Blades of Grass*, and Laureen Marchand for *Adagio for a Difficult Spring*, which led me to "painter" and "Something In You Reaches," respectively.

Steven Ross Smith
Saskatoon. July 1997.

Contents

EVERYTHING WE SEE COULD ALSO BE OTHERWISE.

EVERYTHING WE CAN DESCRIBE AT ALL COULD ALSO BE OTHERWISE.

LUDWIG WITTGENSTEIN

THE READER

i close the book. stare at the black and white image on its glossy cover. an ambiguous image that evokes many possibilities. it's suited to this odd story that leaves me confused. what, exactly, has happened? a character has died, i think, in the bed, under the bedspread, made of a material, the name of which i can't remember. i haven't been remembering well for some time. he might have been killed. might have been dead before the story began. can i be sure the victim is male?... and the woman. was she the killer? the victim? and her perfume, so strong, so sweet.

i slip my hand from the book's spine onto the armrest of the chair. the coarse fabric, rough under my palm, awakens nerve endings. hundreds, thousands. microscopic circuits moving from the skin of my palm, deeper into flesh, up through the shoulder, to the spine, up to the stem and into my brain.

the upholstery on the chair is pinky-red. salmon, the colour's name, i suppose. a rough, looped, manmade fabric popular in the fifties, nylon perhaps. i could verify this by lifting the cushion and searching for a label.

the story disturbed me. overlapping events with an undertone of violence, of sexual tension, and an overtone of isolation. her fingernails so red. encounters, empty of feeling, take place. seem to exist only to manipulate the reader, satisfy the voyeur. why should this bother me? it is, after all, only a story.

my hand lifts from my lap, holding the book. moves toward the walnut table beside my chair. wood with a modest grain, dark stain, high gloss. certainly not oak or cedar, which are not usually stained so dark. no, not walnut either. they'd all be too expensive for this place.

the sky has been darkening for some time. when i began reading, the afternoon sunlight was just beginning to fade. since then the sun must have set in splendid orange and purple hues. or perhaps it disappeared entirely behind a cloud low on the horizon, offering a sickly greying dusk. whatever way, the sunset occurred without my notice. i was absorbed in the story, reading it twice to follow the twists of plot, temporal shifts, and the characters blending into each other's flesh.

i lay down the book. rest it atop the white doily protecting the table's surface. this book will not scratch the finish. the doily is soiled.

what message did the author have in mind? what was the setting? a cocktail party? a bedroom? both? who was in the bed?

my hand hovers over the book. i lower my arm, hand to my lap, fingers brushing the opposite wrist. reminds me of her touch. yes. there on my wrist. she held her thumb there and said you're alive. i feel your heart. feel mine. she offered her wrist to my fingers and we felt each other's heartbeats. together, touching like that and gazing into each other's eyes. the throbbing.

i really must get packing. i have to prepare my belongings for departure. pick up my cleaned shirts from the front desk, call a taxi, get cash from the bank machine. then i'm on my way.

the room seems lonely now, dimmer than when i first arrived. hollow, emptier. maybe it's the colours. colours that drain life. carpet a shade that defies description, perhaps lime aspic. and patterned mustard wallpaper. makes the eyes spin. to think they paid someone to pick these finishings.

provocative? what would be the right word? menacing? i felt aroused at a few points in the story. no. no. impossible. these were not pleasant events. horrible, in fact. why did i keep reading? once you read, you're caught. hooked. you clamber inside the shape the book creates. you're trapped. tricked by every page.

it's been three days now. i told the desk clerk i didn't want to be disturbed for three days. not even to have the bed made up. he peered at me through his thick glasses, his eyes magnified, reptilian. i couldn't tell what he was thinking. perhaps nothing seems odd in a cheap motel.

why would someone leave such a book in a motel room? usually there's just a bible and a phone book. i brought my own reading matter, a couple of newspapers, a magazine, but i cast them aside. what caused her scars?

i should get moving. open the curtain and see if anyone's out there. i hadn't noticed how dingy these curtains are. dirty olive and beige plastic, rain-stained. three days not seeing them. time to move. i should suggest to the clerk that they be cleaned. if they can be. can you clean this kind of petroleum by-product? maybe they're disposable. or flammable. from fire they came, to fire they must return.

one spring, i found a short hunk of stove pipe and trapped a fat green caterpillar, setting the pipe around it like a corral. it crawled from edge to edge, at each barrier probing the metal with its feelers. i liked the colour of that insect, but its undulating bulgy body repulsed me. i'd been reading a book. i tore out the pages. stuffed them in the pipe and caught sunlight in my magnifying glass. the ink made a lot of smoke. when the flames went out i grabbed the pipe. burnt the palms of my hands. a charred clump of caterpillar flesh lay in a circle of brown, a circle of death ringed by green and green. my hands did not heal well. i remember the swish of trees. smoke mingling with the sweet smell of spring lilac.

a backless dress. its dark green shimmer. straps slipping from her pale shoulders. revealing the scars. fabric gliding down her slim hips. pooling at her bare feet stepping out. her waist bending. dress tossed. the satin cool against my face. her head thrown back to loosen her long grey hair with red-tipped fingers. the translucent hollow of her throat.

as if caught in an updraft. lifted from my chair by an allure i can't resist. drift in slow motion toward the bed. falling. falling. collapsing onto the patterned spread. chafing my arms. nubs of fabric poke me through my clothing.

voices. their voices approaching. damn. i should have thrown my things together and left. instead i read. instead i wondered. the thin walls let the sounds in. maybe out. i must be silent. i roll and pull the covers over. reach my hand under the pillow. find it. cold. smooth against nerve endings. so smooth, smoother than skin. gun-metal smooth.

chenille. that's it. the bedspread is chenille.

Ricochet

"Goddammitscold."

We pat the snow from our coats, stamp our feet, head for an empty table. JB shivers behind his scarf.

"Should have waited till summer to die."

"Summer forty years from now." I sit down, pull my arms free, drop my coat onto the chair back. "Never thought I'd get an afternoon off by Gary's doing, he was always working."

"Probably still working wherever he... is." JB gulps the last syllable, as we're swallowed by the dim clatter and cough, the deep green walls, the glint of chrome, black arborite. I look for words to hold the three of us together.

"We were a triangle."

"Whatsat?" JB asks, unwinding his scarf.

"Gary, you, me. We had a shape."

Along one wall runs a scuffed oak bar stained dark, a smoked mirror behind it. Pallid waiters who haven't seen the sun for days glide through the shadowy air. In the far corner, two men, cigarettes lodged in their mouths, bend and step a slow dance in the circle of light around the billiard table to the clack of ricocheting balls.

"You know, JB, Gary was the smartest, smarter than any of us. He knew how to make the most of life. I figured he'd outfox death long after the rest of us had been snared."

"Yeah. Doesn't make sense."

"What'll it be, gentlemen?" The waiter's thin black moustache darts into our lament. JB is quick.

"Draft and a whisky chaser, Irish."

I nod. "Same for me."

"Anything to eat, fellows?"

JB speaks for both of us. "Thanks, no. We're not hungry."

JB's hands rest flat on the table, pale, resigned, the corners of his nails bitten down into red sockets. He studies a point just beyond his fingertips.

"Was thinking... during the service... takes something like this to make you remember."

"Remembering. That's all I've been doing. Faster than I can keep track. Gary kept us moving. He'd come up with a terrific idea, invent a way to do it, get us to carry it out."

"Like publishing the pun calendar."

"Yeah."

JB's mouth curves in a smile that mirrors my own. The smile doesn't reach his dark eyes, and I look away, searching the murky room, seeking a presence among the indistinct customers, mostly men, alone at tables or in twos or threes. Gary will emerge if I look hard enough. If I speak his name.

"Gary... Gary, you, me... a long time. We have to pay more attention."

"How do you mean?" JB reaches toward the whisky snifter, his fingers stopping at first contact with its smooth surface.

"Do things together. Talk. Not be so afraid. Be constructive."

"We've been doing that."

"We have, but we've got to do it... better."

JB fiddles with his snifter, twirling the glass on the table top. I raise my beer.

"Here's to Gary, to friendships that never die."

"To Gary."

The clink of our glasses chimes in the smoky air, echoes back the tinkle and clatter of other glasses, other times. I'm looking for something to anchor me.

"So, JB, should we swear some kind of new allegiance here and now?"

JB says nothing. I study the thinning beer foam, the emptiness.

"Dave, I've been thinking... the opposite."

"What do you mean?"

"That we ought to ease off."

Someone laughs at a nearby table. I look up. JB's face turns mustardy. Sweat breaks on my neck.

"You're joking?"

"Just answering your question, David, straightforward as I bloody can." A muscle pulses in JB's jaw. In. Out.

"Things've changed. May be the time to cut the ties." His angular chin juts.

The waiter pushes a chair to the next table. JB shifts in his seat, waves his finger in a circle to order another round.

"Hold it, JB, I can't drink that much, that fast."

"We're having a few for Gary, remember? I have to drink for all of us now? Waiter, change that," JB calls, "one martini here."

The waiter nods over his shoulder. JB's words scrape in my head, replaying until I speak.

"You're not tied..." Something catches in my throat. "To me, man."

"I don't mean it that way." JB's forehead wrinkles, trying to squeeze out another possibility. Underneath the table my leg cramps.

JB wipes at invisible dust on the arborite. The air in the room, a cloak over my face. I gulp a slug of Irish.

"Gary's gone, and you're flipping out."

"I'm not. Just the connection's not the same. It was always Gary for you. I just happened along."

"What? We were friends. Man, where's this coming from?"

"You don't know? You never did know what I was thinking." JB scratches at the cuticle of his thumb with a fingernail. "Cause I was hardly there to you."

"You're full of shit."

"Maybe. And you, so full of sense. Man, listen to you."

JB throws his martini back in one swallow, olive and all.

We sat at these tables so many times, the three of us. Our friendship planted, grown here. The ground slips. I look into JB's eyes. Moist, widened by the alcohol. Startled. I see this for the first time. I reach across the table. My hand stops short of JB's clenched fist. He stares toward the mirror behind the bar. I concentrate on distance beyond his face. Most of the tables are occupied and JB's words cut into the mumbling voices and background music.

"Oh, hell, Dave. Let's shoot some pool."

"No. This is started. I don't think we can leave it up in the air."

"It's not in the air, it's in my bones, and I can't talk it out." JB says.

"But you're making pronouncements, without giving me... us... any options."

"I'm trying to be... what would you say... constructive."

"Constructive schmuctive. You're destroying what's left."

"Just saying what's what."

"You're blaming me."

"You want to put it that way, okay." JB shrugs, mocking.

I want to grab him. Shake him. I try with words.

"No, you say it. If that's how you feel, say it right out. Tell me, 'it's your fault, Dave, because you were never really my friend, you only cared about Gary.' Say 'that hurts me, Dave.'"

"I did. I did," he says.

JB's hands grab the chair arms. He lifts slightly, turns his body away. His left arm and shoulder angle toward me. He looks away.

"You didn't, JB. You just agreed with what I said."

JB's eyes remain averted.

"I have my own ideas, right? You say they're full of shit. That makes our friendship come up bullshit."

"I didn't say bullshit... you said bullshit. It hasn't all been bull..."

"All, some? Waiter. Double." JB's eyes turn back to me.

"And one for my... acquaintance, no matter what. And David, you bloody well drink." JB chews a fingernail. Silence stretches a raw chord between us. "And stop shouting. I don't need people to know about my personal life."

People at close tables have been looking at us. Pain drills my forehead. I want to scream sense into JB, but I lower my voice.

"They don't know what's going on, JB. It just looks like we're arguing... about politics or something."

"I don't get excited about politics."

"Sure, you do. You've argued with me about politics."

"Yeah, because I'm an asshole."

"I didn't say you were an asshole."

"Everybody's an asshole. Even Gary, fucking off on us with no warning."

"Don't insult him. His memory deserves more than that."

"See, Dave? I give Gary a compliment, make a joke, and you don't understand. You're all proper and logic. So polite. Don't be so fucking sensible. You can't even laugh. Shake your balls once in a while. They won't shatter."

My hands fly across the table, grab JB's shirtfront, push my knuckles to his throat.

"Shut up. I'll show you who's..."

The momentum carries my body forward, pushes JB back, sends the table drinks chairs crashing. We fall, thudding to the floor, debris dropping around us. My ears pound like a freight train. JB's chest rises, falls in quick puffs beneath mine. His arms across my back, our stomachs, hips press together, my thigh between his legs, his foot locked on my ankle. Our bodies immobile, trembling. My mouth and nose pressed against his cheek. Until gruff hands grab me by my arms and hoist me to my feet. A big fellow with a beard. The bouncer. JB is pulled up by the waiter, dropped into a chair beside me.

"Gather your stuff guys, you're out," the bouncer says.

"No, no. It was an accident," I say. "I stood up to go to the john, tripped on my chair leg and knocked everything over. I'm sorry."

"You're hammered."

"No. I'm not. I've been trying to get drunk, but I'm stone sober."

The bouncer leans down, looks right into JB's face.

"That right, buddy? You okay?"

JB grabs a napkin, dabs his wet shirt, says, "We'll pick up."

The waiter uprights the table, signals the busboy, moves away. The bouncer watches us. JB and I bend to pick up scattered utensils and broken glass. The smell of the carpet, a dank bouquet of alcohol, cigarette butts, and feet, rises to greet us. I feel the brush of JB's hairs on mine, and the sharp scent of him, an orange in a lunch bag a few days. He grabs a pepper shaker, and we pull ourselves up. The busboy dabs a damp grey mop round our feet. JB whispers at me.

"Maniac, Dave, that was maniac. You're a dumb fuck, you know, like the rest of us."

"Back off, JB, don't hit my nerve again."

"Fuckhead."

"And do me a favour. Find an original word that isn't swearing once in a while. Call me something nice."

"You don't like Fuckhead. How about Sweetie Pie?" JB grins. "How about just 'FH' for short. We'll be like twins, FH, JB."

My ears go hot. "Whatever makes you happy."

The busboy moves away.

"I'm not happy."

"Have another drink."

"Too sad."

"You bring it on yourself. You started this."

"Shit. You think I do this for fucking fun." JB puts his elbows on the table, leans toward me. "Gary and you were my best friends. It's just, I wasn't yours."

"Were, was. Gary was my friend. He's gone. You and I are. We could have something."

"Okay, so I won't cut out in total."

"JB, you can't leave or stay by degrees, you're on your way... Jesus..."

JB parts his lips, puffs out an extended wisp of air, lowers his gaze to the tabletop, grins.

"Right, Sweetie Pie."

"JB, your timing is... hell, I just don't get it."

"FH... you... I..." Resignation fills JB's voice. "You can't pretend things in and out of life."

My face fills with pressure that concentrates around my eyes. JB lowers his forehead onto his folded knuckles, the crown of his head offered, as if in prayer. I study the soft black strands of hair, try to see through. Something squeezes up over my Adam's apple and becomes words.

"I loved him."

JB doesn't look up.

"Me, too. I love him, too."

In this room, hands lift glasses, cigarettes poise below smoke curls in pools of light. Each person, a secret in a veil of skin. Above the bar, the television flashes torsos, happy faces, heady beer, into the sombre air.

A sharp clack splits the din, ricochets in rapid-fire. A triangle breaks. Balls scatter on the green felt of the billiard table.

Without a word, JB gets up. Slips on his coat. Flips his scarf around his neck. Our eyes connect in the space between us. JB scoops a fistful of peanuts from a basket on the next table, stuffs them in his pocket. Shrugs. Moves toward the door.

Goddammitscold.

BLUE HEAVEN

The air inside the plastic membrane is so wet it drips onto her. Close and wet, hot and stinking with chemicals. Yet, as she waters, plucks and turns the plants, she pauses, fingers one blossom and tilts it toward her.

"Rosa," says Gomez the foreman, "don't linger over one plant when many more need your attention."

Rosa squeezes the trigger on the hose nozzle, directs the soft spray over the flowers. Rosa is not her real name, she is Rigoberta Garcia. But she likes *Rosa*, the name an honour bestowed on her by the other women because of her special love for each and every blossom growing here. Though thousands wait for her loving touch, she often stands transfixed by one, in a special moment of communion. When the workers in the greenhouse speak her name, *Rosa*, they know they address her person and her singular passion at the same time. But it is not only Rosa's love that nurtures each blossom to perfection. Many women, like her, care for the growing plants, and the men in white coats do the breeding. The results are stunning, roses and carnations and chrysanthemums unfurling in a lush carpet that, in Rosa's imagination, is like the pathway to heaven.

Rosa and the rest have become used to the regular spraying of chemicals that kills the bugs that might harm the plants. In fact, it is Rosa and her friends Alaide and Maria, who carry out most of the chemical dousing. Rosa holds her breath as much as possible, and sometimes she wears a kerchief over her mouth. But she can often taste the chemicals in her throat many hours after the long bus ride back to the town, and on her lips when she kisses her children. Sometimes in the night she feels sick. But she always gets up for work in the morning. At home her children call her *Mama* and her neighbours call her *Berti*.

Cheryl studies the mirror carefully, slipping her feet into plastic patent pumps, too high to be practical considering the amount of walking she'll have to do, and she is pleased by the shape they give her calves, the length of her legs, dramatized by the dark hose leading to the hem of her black skirt, just short enough to attract attention. Showing a little leg helps sell the roses. Tucked at her trim waist, a white rayon blouse with its collar open reveals a glimpse of neckline and adds a provocative touch beneath her black jacket. The red artificial rose in her lapel brings a wink to her eye as she turns from the mirror to set her mind to her job.

On her way out of the bedroom, she blows a kiss, whispers *Love you* to her daughter Jasmine, asleep in her bed. Says goodbye to the babysitter. She moves gingerly down the steps toward her rusty Civic, chugging to warm up at the curbside. On a strip of ice at the edge of the sidewalk, Cheryl's foot slips and she falls forward, her hands slapping on the cold tin of the car roof. *Shit, just about took a nose dive,* she says under her breath. Placing her feet carefully, she braces herself, works her way around the car to the driver's side door, and eases onto the vinyl seat. The cold pricks at the backs of her thighs and knees. Her breath clouds the inside of the window. Shivering, she flicks on the defrost fan and waits for the window to clear before she pulls away, heading for the warehouse to pick up the roses.

Alicia Morrow sets the crystal wine glass in place at the dining table. She adjusts a napkin, and checks to be certain that nothing is forgotten. The navy blue tablecloth is punctuated by eight place settings with stone grey plates and gleaming silverware. The effect is as fine as the features of her face, as striking as her blue-green eyes, as impeccable as the groomed sweep of her shiny dark hair. Condiments are in place. One bottle of Pouilly-Fume rests in a sterling silver cooler, and beside it, on a white napkin, a bottle of fine Beaujolais sits ready to be uncorked to breathe. And in the centre, a blue Sevres china vase awaits its bouquet. Alicia has been anticipating this dinner for weeks. She has considered and planned each meticulous detail. The menu, the setting, the dress she will wear, the particular ambience she seeks. Instead of a large formal table, Alicia has set a table of modest size, intimate and cosy, to create a close and relaxed tone. She likes to surprise her guests with taste and difference. Her anticipation is keen. At this moment she cannot imagine a table more elegant than her own.

Rosa has been working at the greenhouse for four years now, ever since the disappearance of Jorge, her husband, who left her life one night in mysterious circumstances. She does not believe the story the officials told her, that he got drunk and ran off to Medellin with a prostitute. As she has said often, "He's never left my heart." Alone in her bed at night, she still grieves for him. The rest of the time, her children and her work occupy her thoughts and wishes. She knows that nature has provided her country with bounty, knows that the soil is rich with nutrients for the roses, and that this has provided her with work and some means. But she cannot understand why there is so little of this bounty left over for her family. She dreams of a place where her children, Federico, Gloria, and Enrique, can grow and bloom in great beauty, a kind of greenhouse for children, but without chemicals.

"I'll take five dozen, Frank," Cheryl says, digging into her purse.

"That all, girl?" asks Frank, a hint of the salesman in his voice.

"I don't think it's going to be a big night. Last night I lost money with four dozen. Too many left over."

"It's Friday, usually your best night," he prompts.

"It's bloody cold, and Christmas is just done. Nobody's got any cash left," says Cheryl.

"Take six dozen, just in case."

"That's thirty-six dollars. I only got thirty-three, and I need some for change."

"Tell you what. I'll give you a break," says Frank, "take six dozen for your thirty-three bucks, and I'll lend you some change, if you'll deliver this special order for me. Already paid for. Two dozen beauties going to Forest Heights for 8:15 sharp, address on the box. The Morrow woman'll give you a tip. Guaranteed. But be on time, and keep the roses in the box. It's insulated. Don't open it and don't leave it out in the cold."

"All right, all right. But if I lose money, Frank, I'm cutting back from here on. I can't afford to work for nothing. I got a kid to feed."

Cheryl pockets the change and loads the six dozen flowers into her styrofoam cooler. She hefts the box with the gold ribbon under one arm, picks up the cooler and heads out.

After the door closes behind her, Frank tallies up the cash.

"Two-fifty, two-sixty, two-hundred-and-sixty five."

He buys from a South American importer, supplies the shops in town with carnations, roses and chrysanthemums. Occasionally he takes the odd special order. What he has left over, he sells to nighthawkers like Cheryl, Wednesday through Saturday, cash up front, six bucks a dozen.

"A pretty good wad of tax-free cash," he says to himself, flicking off the light, "especially for flowers I'd otherwise be throwing in the bin."

Alicia Morrow wants to be certain that her hired servers will understand and enhance the ambience she seeks for the dinner.

"Merna, Betty," she says, "I know you're professionals, but there are a few things I'd like to make you aware of. You'll notice this is a small table. I want to create an intimate informal atmosphere tonight, kind of cosy, but elegant. Don't draw unnecessary attention to your presence. But I don't mean you have to be robotic." Alicia laughs. "If a guest addresses you, don't be afraid to respond, smile, whatever, if appropriate. But don't hover. The order of dishes, the timing and preparation is written on a card beside the stove."

"No need to worry, Ms. Morrow," says Merna. Betty nods in affirmation.

"Good. Any questions about the food, speak to Franz. I may assist you from time to time, just to emphasize the informal tone."

"Certainly."

"And Julie Garnette, the harpist from the symphony, will play before dinner, and she'll do a small concert during dessert. You'll bring the second round of coffee with armagnac as people are finishing the creme caramel, and Julie will begin to play. Don't serve again until she's done. All right?"

"Yes, ma'am," they say in unison.

"That's all for now."

Alicia watches the crisp black-and-white uniforms disappear through the kitchen door. She imagines that she has found the perfect way to celebrate her appointment to board of directors of the symphony. A stylish gathering of a few key supporters. Her eyes turn to the table, to the empty Sevres vase. Rather than sprays of floral arrangements throughout the room, she has chosen the singular but dramatic gesture of two dozen roses, delivered fresh, just after the arrival of her guests. Special roses, which will show her unique and exquisite taste, and create a bit of surprise. She speaks, as if to an absent companion, "This will be a memorable occasion."

Rosa has seen two unusual things. One is the snake turning in circles in the clearing in the forest. The other is the sores on her hands and under her arms that do not heal. Even the milk of the aloe plant does not help.

"Was the snake eating its tail, Rigoberta?" asks Jacinto.

"If it was, wouldn't this be an omen?" asks Rosa.

"It depends. But you have answered my question with another question."

"I didn't mean to. You know me. I'm curious. I have my own ideas," she says. "But I respect yours, Senor Jacinto. No, the snake didn't seem to eat its tail, but to follow it."

"If the snake eats its tail, this can mean destruction, perhaps self-destruction. However, it can also mean rejuvenation. Or both at the same time. The circumstances are important. But a snake turning circles going nowhere, Rosa, is a bad omen."

"A sign for me alone, Senor?"

"Yes. Only you have seen this. It is a sign to you."

"What can I do?" Rosa asks.

"I can make you no promises, but you must find a shed snake skin and hang it over your door on your first day of menses. And question what you have done to deserve ill fortune. Then ask for forgiveness. Perhaps the circle will open."

Rosa knows where the snakes live, and knowing she will bleed soon, she hunts there after leaving Jacinto. While she hunts, she wonders whether she should have told Senor Jacinto of her sores, as she knows she must, in order to be cured. She reminds herself to always wear the rubber gloves for protection in the greenhouse, and to continue to work hard, even when the pain from the sores is strong.

Finally she finds a shed skin. A few days later she nails it above her door.

Cheryl holds the styrofoam cooler with one arm and one raised knee, swings open the big oak door with the other hand, sidles, bouncing the door off her hip and pushing the box ahead into the low-key lighting and the din of conversations of the tavern. She sets the box against the wall, opens it, lifts out a bouquet, lays it across the crook of her elbow. She extracts two roses from the cluster, passes through the archway into the familiar cloud of smoke, alcohol and voices. She approaches the first table, a group of boisterous men and women, and offers, with a smile.

"A rose for your table. Only a dollar-fifty each or twelve dollars for the dozen."

"How 'bout a kiss for a rose, doll?"

Cheryl holds the two roses between her and the customer.

"Sorry, sir, it's only the roses for sale, a dollar-fifty each." She turns away and moves along.

Cheryl figures she's had all the responses possible, and now she can see them coming before they're offered. The ignorers, the automatic-decliners, the bashful-romantic-buyers, the I'll-help-you-out-buyers, and a variety of others. The ratios are always more or less the same. But she doesn't second-guess. She approaches every table, just in case. A sale is a sale.

"A red rose here, please," calls the young man sitting next to a shyly smiling woman. Cheryl offers her bouquet.

"Here, choose your own, miss."

"Thank you," she says, reaching.

As the man slips Cheryl the change, the woman plants a kiss on the cheek of her gallant. Cheryl smiles, glances at her watch.

"Eight o'clock. Special delivery time," she says, angling toward the door.

Alicia's guests have arrived. Camille Doucet, the political fund-raiser; Milton Cranley, criminal lawyer; Doctor Mildred Preece, neuro-surgeon; and their companions. Julie Garnette plays Saint-Saëns on the harp; Alicia glides from guest to guest, graceful and gracious. She offers the silver tray with canapés, artichoke rounds with caviar, and Merna and Betty follow with the Pouilly-Fume, and smoked salmon crescents.

Alicia approaches Milton and Nora Cranley and Doctor Preece standing near the harp, listening intently. She offers the tray around.

"Delicious," Cranley whispers, reaching for a second morsel. The others, biting into the delectable hors d'oeuvres, nod in enthusiastic agreement.

Alicia smiles, mimes, "Thank you."

She moves to the other guests, grouped in the study by the fireplace. Here, they are able to watch and hear Julie Garnette through the wide archway, while speaking in hushed tones. They raise their glasses toward Alicia in an informal toast. She does a mock curtsy, and offers more canapés. Alicia is most happy and natural in such a setting. She thrives on it. She is a stylish and charming host, and each guest feels special to be in her company. They savour that feeling, and an ambience that is lush, generous and warm. Just as Alicia has imagined.

Rosa worries about the chemicals. She wonders exactly what they are and whether they might hurt people, even though they help the flowers. They do not have the sweetish smell of chicoloro salve, which relieves the itch of insect bites. The chemical odour is different in a way she cannot explain, an unpleasant way.

"I don't like the chemicals," she says one day at lunch, to the women sitting outside the hothouse, under the eucalyptus tree. "I don't think it's good for us to be inside after the spraying. We should ask to spray at the end of the day, just before we leave."

"Gomez might not like this," says Alaide. "He likes to tell us what to do, not to be told."

"He bosses because he is bossed," says Rosa. "But sometimes he's in the greenhouse when we spray. It would be better for him, too."

"But his boss, who comes each week, tells him what to do," Alaide says. "Gomez wouldn't speak back to him, I'm certain. But, you know that some factories have unions to protect workers like us."

"Don't say that word, Alaide. You know it brings trouble. Even if we think about this, even if we wish to have such a thing, we mustn't say the word."

Rosa has heard that word, *union*, from Jorge's mouth, and she knows the implications. And Rosa knows that Jorge didn't drink and run off with a prostitute, but he did go to meetings, and when Rosa asked about them, he would only raise his hand to his lips and narrow his eyes, a sign that Rosa should ask no more. And she did not. Yet she knew what she pretended not to know, that he was organizing a union to fight for better wages and conditions for the workers.

"Senoras," Gomez' voice cuts the warm afternoon air. "Have you forgotten your work? Don't you need the plata at the end of the week? Vamos! We must tend and spray."

In silence the women roll up their mesh bags, toss their food scraps into the brush, and head back toward the humid arc of the hothouse.

At the door, which Gomez holds open, Rosa pauses and says, "We don't think you should spray until the end of the day, when we are leaving. It would be better for our health, Senor Gomez."

"I see. Who is the we you speak of, Senora Garcia?"

"I'm sorry, I meant to say I. I feel this."

"If this job isn't good for you, Rosa, perhaps you should consider one that's better for your health. But here we must think of the flowers. The roses, the carnations, the chrysanthemums. They provide our living. What's good for the flowers is good for you, good for us."

"Yes, but we could change something a little and it would still be good for the roses and good for us."

"And do the other women agree with you?"

"I only speak for myself."

"So it's only your health that concerns you."

"No, Senor, everyone's. Even yours."

"You're most generous. But we're wasting time. Be generous with the plants, Rigoberta, and everything will be all right. But don't be so generous with your tongue. What we do now makes everyone a few pesos. We don't want to lose that. Your children couldn't afford to have you lose that, could they? And Rosa, could you live each day without touching, smelling, and gazing upon these gorgeous blossoms?"

Rosa becomes aware of the sting of the broken skin under her arms. She senses the scent of the chemical, even though it is not yet being sprayed. She loses her ground, feels dizzy.

"You're right, Senor Gomez. There are things I couldn't live without. Thank you for listening to me."

Gomez closes the door behind Rosa and turns to walk to the old trailer that is his office. On the way up the worn path, he lifts his hat, draws his wrist across his forehead, and puts the hat back on, pulling the brim low over his brow. His eyes squint with the pressure of thought.

Cheryl pushes the doorbell and cradles the long white box with gold ribbon as if it contained something living, something to be protected. As she waits she wonders how some people can afford their circumstances. How they can pay for a big, ornate brass lamp at their front door that must cost at least as much as she makes in three weeks. The door opens. Billowing toward her on a crest of warm light is a delicious waft of food and soft music. And extending a hand is a radiant woman in a cerulean dress with a soft sheen, off-the-shoulder fit, and full skirt. Cheryl stands, staring.

"Good, my flowers. Perfect. "

"Oh, yes. Miss Morrow. Your roses." Cheryl presents the box. "It's already paid..."

The woman smiles graciously.

"Yes, I know. And you're right on time. Thank you. Here's something extra."

Cheryl feels the poke of a paper corner in her palm as the door closes and she's left in the yellow glow of the lantern. She steps back and looks down at a white envelope in her hand. She clutches it and walks to the car. Once in the seat she opens the envelope and pulls out a twenty-dollar bill.

"Wow..." she says, her voice trailing off under the whoosh of the heater fan. Looking toward the house, through the front window, she sees poised, fashionable people standing and moving in the bright room. Their shapes have a definite outline. Shoulders, waists, arms, nodding heads. "People like that stand in front of windows in rooms and know who they are," she thinks. She takes one last look, wheels the car from the curb onto the roadway and turns toward downtown.

Alicia sets the box on the sideboard. Her guests chat and laugh, drinks in hand, but she knows they are aware of her. The clear melodic notes of the harp float amidst the conversation. Mildred Preece approaches her.

"A surprise? Can I help?"

"Certainly."

Alicia lifts the box lid.

"Oh, my. They're gorgeous," says Dr. Preece as the silvery-lilac heads of twenty-four roses come into view, set off against deep green leaves. "What a surprising colour."

"They're Blue Heavens, my favourites. I have them imported. I think of them as having the colour of veins in a wrist."

"So they do," says the doctor, "I should know."

Alicia laughs.

"Here, I'll hold the vase. Why don't you set them in?"

Dr. Preece reaches in and slips one hand under the blossoms, and the other under the stems.

"Ouch." She withdraws her hand and sucks briefly on a bit of flesh. "A thorn. Sharp devil." She reaches back in and lifts the Blue Heavens from the box. A sudden touch, moist and soft, slithers along her forearm. The feeling lingers even as the snake slips off at her elbow onto the sideboard and drops over the edge. Dr. Preece stares. Alicia blinks unbelievingly. For a second or an eternity, the two women could not say which, they do not move or speak. Then the roses fly in all directions and the air explodes with their screams.

The guests rush in from the living room, surrounding the two women. Dr. Preece stares at her hand. Two pin pricks side by side where the thumb joins the palm ooze tiny drops of blood, the tissue a reddening circle surrounded by white.

Cheryl hands the two young women a rose each, as they pass her three dollars and offer the roses to their dates. The men take them self-consciously, making jokes, uncertain how to handle such a gift.

"Sniff it," says the blonde.

"Put it in your hair, just over your ear," says the brunette. The young men handle the flowers awkwardly and everyone laughs, Cheryl chuckling, too, as she moves to the next table.

"How many you got left?" asks the raspy voice.

"Six," says Cheryl, automatically on her guard.

"I'll take 'em all, if you throw yourself into the bargain." Before she can move away, his hand reaches and grabs her wrist. Clenched in his grip, she pulls back. His arm stretches out with her and she looks directly at his face, at his defiant eyes, his grinning teeth, his cocky chin pointed up at her, the sweat on his neck, his broad shoulders, and the tattoo. The tattoo, blue lines, red and green patterns coiling from his biceps around his forearm, down to the back of his hand, where an open jaw and flicking tongue threaten, as his big knuckles flex, fingers shackling her thin flesh and bone.

Following her eyes, he says, "Pretty, eh? I'd like to have you wound around me just like that. You'd like my... bite." Cheryl's wrist burns in the squeeze of his grip.

"Tell you what," she says. "I'll give you more than one break." She leans down, looking in his eyes, aware that she's exposing the depth of her cleavage. She sees his eyes shift from her face. She continues, "Half price, volume discount... Let go now, so I can sit down."

His grip eases and she moves toward the chair as if to sit. She pauses, lays the half dozen roses on the table. Leans low again.

"Get out your money. Four-fifty. And keep an eye on the roses... on the roses, I said," Cheryl smiles, winks. "I'll be right back."

As she walks away, he watches the sway of her hips, admires the fine curve of her legs, turns and winks to a buddy, slides his tongue across his lips. Cheryl rounds the corner to the washroom, walks past, out the back door.

Rosa does not feel well this morning. There is no energy in her body, and the sores cause a dull discomfort, as if there is something growing under her skin. She manages to get herself up to tend to the children's breakfast and send Gloria and Federico, the two oldest, off to school. When they're gone, she takes Enrique two doors away to Ana's house.

"Ana, will you please take care of my boy for a while? I'm not feeling well. My time, you know, and the sores. I need an extra hour or two in bed."

This done, Rosa walks back toward the house. At the end of the street she notices a stranger leaning on a car, his foot up on the shiny bumper, elbow on his knee, cigarette in curved fingers at his lips. The man is looking down the street in her direction. The sun stings. *Too hot for morning*, she thinks. Rosa pushes open her blue door. Her eyes lift to the dry snake skin above the doorway. She passes beneath it and enters the shade of her house, now cool and quiet, and lies down on her bed.

PAINTER

she loses herself in her paint. it is as if the paint reaches out and grabs
her. the chemical smell of acrylic pulling at her. the yield and spring
of the canvas under her fingers and brush pulses in harmony with
her body. in the rose and violet hues she sees her blood stream. lines
are branches, veins, or roads she travels. she relaxes into the colours.
the feel underfoot of the studio's concrete floor softens. overhead,
fluorescent light drifts through the opening roof. she becomes the
movement her body makes, and only this. it is this forgetting of the
self she loves. she becomes less aware the longer she works. it is not
a state she can easily comment on, or remember. so completely is
she lost that she does not notice the sticky fluid rising around her
ankles, nor the taut canvas walls that press toward her. her hands
dance over the flat rectangular surface. paint slips into the tiny and
infinitely repeating crevasses in the weave. a breeze picks up in the
forest. spruce trees swish and whisper. birch and poplar rustle in the
passing currents of air. she doesn't hear the barking of the barred
owl. doesn't see its eyes peering down from the branch outside the
window. she doesn't hear a voice calling her name from the other
side of the creek.

the brush and colours speak to her.
   "over here."
   "stronger."
   "just a dab."
   "more sweep."

"thin, now thick."

she responds to the cues. some colours seek power, want to take over. some, self-effacing, move rapidly to backgrounds. some want to hurt.

"scrape me."

"jab me."

"bind me among the others."

she does as she feels. cannot separate demand from desire. arousal. her whole body growing moist. fire moving from her fingertips and arms. into her chest. down through her stomach. and into thighs. for her there is no face in the trees. no voice across the river. she does not hear the scream pouring from her own throat.

his eyes dart back and forth. the woods are dense and alive. they are not black or brown, grey or muted silver. everywhere the shades of blood. the way it looks under the microscope. the forest, crimson-pink. he cannot stop himself from moving toward this light's radiant source. pulsing, pink, translucent, filling his vision. above his head, an unseen owl calls. the scent in the air, familiar. musk. fear. a sting in his eyes. metallic taste in his mouth. someone calls his name. he pauses, listens. a trick of the wind. he continues, the forest floor spongy under his careful walk.

her arms push. jerk erratically. she is near exhaustion. she slips in the paint's slick texture. she has fought the colours a long time. they have crawled into her eyes. under her fingernails. into her nostrils. they run across her twisting stomach. spill over erect nipples. colour each hair. each pore. she is torn between fear and arousal. fighting. giving in. struggling and succumbing. she thrusts and grasps. is pressed and bound in the canvas. her throat opening. nothing but air moving from her oesophagus, past the still uvula, over her tongue, through clenched teeth and over her tight lips. air. no sound. nothing but air. her fevered breathing. her eyes wide open. unmoving in a sea of pale red.

peering in from the doorway he sees the room filled with colour. pulsing and coursing red. the centre of the heart. the intensity pushes him back. he resists. recovering, he enters. a large painting hangs on the wall. facing the door. emanates into the whole space. vibrant. the crystal heart of pink granite. the underside of freshly skinned rabbit hide. the inside of a rose petal. possibilities hover in his mind, an elusive pushing and poking at consciousness. remaining out of grasp. between the blades of grass, or branches, veins or cracks, he remains uncertain.

his eye is caught. a figure slips among the densities of pigment. paler than its surroundings. he moves closer. blinks. sees a body in the painting. no. nothing. the close air. he looks away. wipes his brow in time to see a brush roll from the table and drop to the concrete floor. a crimson patch grows around the bristles, as its wet paint pools onto the floor. an owl screeches. he leans closer to the painting. the blades dance. brushed by something passing.

he steps back. a voice calls his name. a touch on his hand. he turns. movement on the surface of the painting. he sees her. they are both running naked through dense forest. a rose thorn catches his flesh. a small circle of blood forms on his thigh. drips a pinkish streak down to his knee. she is panting, panicked. her hands are bound with twine. a strip of canvas covers her mouth. she stumbles, falls toward a thistle bush. he grabs her. pulls her aside. they fall in slow motion. their eyes turn to watch the mauve thistle flowers float upward as they fall past. her back crushes into the soft bed of spruce needles and birch leaves. he lands on his hands and knees. is over her. crouching above her prone body. tears flowing from her eyes. her breathing laboured. her smell is strong. chemical. he lifts his hand to her bindings. slips the twine from her wrists, the canvas from her mouth.

"you're all right now," he says. "you're safe."

"it was the painting," she whispers.

he pauses. "i know."

she trembles. "someone was calling me."

he assures her, "it wasn't me."

she exhales, relieved.

"how long have you been bound?"

"until now," she replies.

he continues, "it's okay, it's new to me, i'm still outside it. relax."

she breathes deeply, whispers, "i don't know any other way. it takes over."

in a low voice he says, "it was bright. crimson. repulsive and attractive at the same time."

"the duality," she offers.

"the pull," he answers. "the blood and the rose."

"don't get metaphorical," she insists.

he lowers his lips towards hers. before they meet, he whispers, "it's about giving up, loss, sacrifice."

"is this a seduction?" she asks.

"no, i mean giving up in order to create."

"who are you?" she asks.

"you already know," he replies.

"yes," she responds, pulling closer, surrendering.

instinctively, in that moment before complete awakening, they slide toward each other's warmth, in tender embrace. dawn filters rosy-coloured light through the slatted bamboo blinds. they awaken on the straw japanese mat beside the painting, each completely raw, protective shells cracked open. they kiss. the smell of acrylic paint hangs in the close air of the studio. the scent of lovemaking clings to them. he slips out of bed and scrambles toward the bathroom.

through the door she hears running water. over it he calls her name. drifting, she does not respond. he calls. she hears only the dawn birds and swishing trees. he calls again, louder, jarring her from the overwhelming hug of sleep.

"what?" she asks.

through the door he shouts, "it's daylight. i've got to be on my way."

"and i've got to get back to the painting." she props up on one elbow to look at the work. "i like it," she says aloud, as he returns.

"pardon?" he asks.

"oh, i was talking to myself. i said, 'i like it.'"

"what, our sex?"

"yes, but i meant my painting."

"i like it, too. they're the same. passion, the bloodstream, the pink centre of the heart."

"it's not that," she says, "it's the crimson grass. it's all there."

"ah, abstraction," he says.

"reality," she counters.

AFTER THE NEWS

Suzanne Varley carries a laundry basket to the foot of the stairs. Her husband David, glancing up from doing the dishes in the kitchen, flips the tea towel over his shoulder, tiptoes behind her, puts his arms around her waist and kisses the nape of her neck. She shrugs her shoulders and leans back into him.

"Come sit down, watch the news with me," he says.

"I'd love to, but I'm too tired. The bank was busy, and the kids have worn me out. It's been a long day. I want to fold this laundry, then go to bed."

"I'm tired too," says David, "but I want to check in on the world."

She and David often snuggle on the couch at news time, finally able to take advantage of being alone.

"Tomorrow night, David. For sure."

"I'll hold you to that, Suzie-Q."

Suzanne kisses David on the forehead. He puts his hand on the small of her back and moves his lips to hers, kissing with passion, real but over-acted. She bends back, in a mock swoon. Their lips part to chuckles from each of them.

"Save some for our rendezvous, Casanova," she says, "now it's time for good night."

He winks. "Till we meet again. Night, darlin'." He turns toward the living room.

Suzanne picks up the laundry basket and heads upstairs. He grabs the remote control and flicks on channel twelve.

"Keep the volume down, so you don't wake Bobby and Jennifer," Suzanne calls back down the stairs. "G'night."

David Varley enjoys routine. It is a relaxing contrast to his work as a paramedic. At this time every night, after reading a story to the children, he settles in, with or without Suzanne, to the television news. Even though he says that the news is always the same six stories renewed by changing characters and locations.

1. NOLAND ROBINSON, HEAD & SHOULDERS. IN STUDIO.	NOLAND ROBINSON: (SYNC): Good evening. Noland Robinson, at the anchor desk. Tonight's top stories . . .

Jennifer sleeps, deep in a dream about *him*, and it feels so good. He's holding her hand across the table at the A&W, and saying he likes her Benetton sweater. She's in love. They go to the school dance, and everyone stands back staring at them. He and Jennifer dance as if they're all alone. She tingles when he holds her so close.

Bobby is awake, whispering to his pet cat, Snuffles.

"I'm an astronaut flying above the world in a rocket. Everything small way down below me. Dark out here except for sparking stars. My squadron follows behind. I'm the captain. We're searching for you, Snuffles. You got loose from our station and you're floating in space. Good thing you sneeze a lot. We're following your sound. Don't worry, Snuffles. We'll rescue you."

Suzanne decides to skip the laundry folding and go right to bed. As she changes into her pyjamas, her mind drifts. *Maybe when David turns in, I'll wake up, roll over and hold him close. Perhaps we'll make love.*

She smiles, lifts a corner of the sheets and slips in, pulling the covers up to her neck.

Transfixed by the pixillated light of the television screen and settled on the comfortable leather couch, David travels through the news world of murder, war and starvation. When a loud commercial breaks the spell, he gets up and heads for the refrigerator for a glass of milk.

In afterglow, Jennifer is still dancing. She has woken up, and she feels the feeling of being a graceful dancer in his arms. It all seems so real in the dark and she can see his sexy eyes looking at her from the poster on the wall. She hears the fridge door close, and the sound of the TV, very low.

In space Bobby worries there won't be enough air for Snuffles to breathe. He gets scared by his own game.

He calls out, "Snuffles."

"Mmrrrff," the cat answers.

He reaches out and touches her, beside him on the bed.

A loud knock makes David jump out of his chair. The thump enters Suzanne's drift into slumber. A thud, like a wooden mallet, at the front door. *At this hour?* thinks David, half in uncertainty and half in annoyance. *Damn. This'll wake up Suzie and the kids.* He hurries to the door. Suzanne listens in the darkness, begins reaching for her housecoat.

David opens the door a crack and meets a surprise at eye level— a gun barrel. He jams his shoulder against the door as a hand reaches around and grabs him by the shirt. SNAP. At the sound, Suzanne switches on the light, slips on her housecoat. Voices. The repetitive beat of hurrying feet in the hall, then on the stairs.

Maybe, thinks Jennifer, *it's the telegram man with news that I won the date with him.*

Bobby hears the noise downstairs. He hugs Snuffles, who tries to get away.

"David," calls Suzanne, dashing out of the bedroom. Three men rush her at the top of the stairs, waving guns. The first puts a shoulder into her, knocking her over. The second stops, points his rifle at her forehead. A blur of battle fatigues, gun muzzle, and hard eyes.

"Is it true? Daddy, did I really win?" Jennifer calls.

"JENNIFER, BOBBY." Suzanne shouts.

"Shut up!" he hisses, clench-teethed, from inside a black balaclava.

"Daddy!" Jennifer calls toward the door as it bursts open.

The door crashes open to Bobby's room and a person grabs him. Carries him out.

"Snuffles!"

The rifle barrel gouges Suzanne's shoulder. A thug dressed in black pushes past her, shoving Jennifer ahead. Another lugs Bobby under his arm. Suzanne squirms.

"You leave..."

A flat pop rings in her ears.

"Mom!" calls Jennifer.

"JENN, BOBBY."

Suzanne's shoulder feels like a hot iron is pressed to it.

Bobby cries out: "MUMMY!... DADDY!... SNUFFLES!"

Jennifer turns to run back toward her Mom. A rifle butt cracks her jaw, drops her in her tracks. Suzanne pushes up on one elbow. Her guard pushes his fist into her mouth. She bites the knuckle. He drops a knee to her chest, punches her to the floor, jams the snout of the gun barrel between her teeth, presses it to the back of her throat. He holds the gun with one hand, with the other rips her housecoat and nightgown open. Bobby lies at the bottom of the stairs, whimpering. Suzanne twists, grabs the gun barrel, pushes it from her mouth, rolls, kicking at her captor's crotch, screaming. BANG!

Everything blurs before David's opening eyes, his thumping head. Putting his hand to the pain in his leg, he feels a warm, sticky mush. He squints. He's lying in a shambles. The television glows with static and snow that rolls upward repetitively. A whistling tone pierces the air. Lamps pushed over, table upended, books kicked about, smashed glass on the floor.

"My god!" He tries to get to his feet, topples. His leg is mashed, bleeding with a big wound. *Shotgun,* he thinks. He crawls along the carpet toward the stairs, pulling with his hands and arms.

"SUZANNE, BOBBY, JENNIFER!"

No answer.

"What the fuck's going on?"

He looks over his shoulder, expecting to see someone hammering on his leg, but all he sees is the crimson clot on his pants and a faint streak on the carpet. The top of the stairs swirls like a midway ride. He pulls himself up a step. And another.

"SUZANNE! SUZANNE!"

She lies on the carpet a few feet ahead. Legs and breasts uncovered. He crawls to her. Blood pools on the floor behind her head and shoulder. Her still mouth torn, swollen, her eyes wide open. David's lips tighten over his teeth, the veins in his neck enlarge as if he were screaming. He clutches her to him. Holding.

He lays her gently down, pushes himself up by leaning on the wall.

"BOBBY, JENNY."

First room, Bobby's— gone, then Jennifer's— gone. David hobbles back along the hall wall, hops down the stairs, clutching the banister. Through the dining room doors he spots Jennifer's bicycle in the back yard.

"I'll find them. I'll find them, Suzanne."

ANNOUNCER:

Good evening. This is 'As It Is,' CKQJ Radio's direct connection to events around the world. I'm Daryll Bruce, and tonight we've got trouble spots, star stops, environmental bits, and sports hits, so stay with us. To start off, a special report from Bruce's *Notes from the Underground.*

MUSIC STING

DARYLL BRUCE:

Hello, Commander. You won't reveal your name, so we'll call you Commander A.

COMMANDER A:

Yes, sir.

DARYLL BRUCE:

As the leader of the U.R.B. guerrillas, you are engaged in a prolonged struggle, a series of skirmishes that erupt any place, any time, without notice. You define the battle zone. Is this a new kind of war? Domestic war?

COMMANDER A:

It is war, just war.

DARYLL BRUCE:

What is it like for the men and women who are your soldiers to attack their own communities?

COMMANDER A:

It is dirty work. But you must get dirty in order to get clean. In the dirt you have few choices. But these poor had no choices before. We were already at war, but the war against us was surreptitious, undeclared. Survival forces choice. Our choice is to fight back. We tried political means. It didn't work. Street fighting is our last resort. We are noticed now. And we're different from the ruling war machine. We're not slick, but we're effective. We're organized, but we're not a bureaucracy, so we can strike fast. And we have little to lose.

David eases the bike unsteadily along the side of the house to the street. Eerie darkness, streetlamps shot out, flames flaring up here and there. Air full of smoke. A car on fire in the street. People running back and forth. A vehicle backfires, maybe a gunshot. BOOM. The front windows of a house on the crescent blow out. A woman wails, runs through the door into the street.

"JENNIFER! BOBBY!" David calls, the driveway gravel scuffing underfoot.

"EDDY, PATRICIA!" He shouts to the next-door neighbours' open front door. No one comes out. He rolls onto the road, turns toward the corner, pushing with his good leg, pain cutting with each movement. Smoke stings his eyes. Nothing holds still—fence, roadway, grass, houses. On the road ahead, a small shape. He pushes hard to its side. Drops off the bike, onto both knees, nearly blacks out with pain.

"BOBBY!" he shrieks, turning the boy's head to him. Bobby's face looks like he's asleep, a trickle of blood from his mouth. No breath passes his lips.

2. NOLAND ROBINSON,
IN STUDIO, HEAD & SHOULDERS. NOLAND ROBINSON (SYNC):

> We move immediately to a live on-location report from Harry Lund in downtown Toronto.

3. REPORTER: ANNEX IN BG. NEWS REPORTER, HARRY LUND: (SYNC):

> A charming and quiet neighbourhood in downtown Toronto went from tranquillity to terror in a flash late last night. The Annex has been turned into a war zone.

David wobbles up the street on the bike, his leg propelling him with small weak strokes, his arms fighting to keep the wheel straight, body slumped low over the handle bars, pushing into the smoke and noise, unaware of his course, eyes glazed, pain surging through him as if he's being squeezed in a vice. Mumbling.

"This is my home... I mow the lawn... I grow tomatoes in the yard... kiss my kids goodnight... hold Suzanne to me in the dark... we are free... this..."

Boots, boots running, shouts, a crackle...

4. HARRY LUND O/C

HARRY LUND: (SYNC):
Guerrillas from the western
sector of the city have
occupied the Annex in an

5. EXPLOSIONS OF LIGHT, BG.

attempt to gain a foothold
downtown. No one knows how
they came to be present in such
numbers before invading and
sealing off the Annex.
Specialists believe they may
have been brought into the zone
in transport trailers in the
daytime. As many as thirty
trucks may have been parked
before the curfew in various
parts of the large central
neighbourhood. It appears they
took residents by surprise
around 1:00 a.m. It is not known
how many have been killed or
wounded, or how much damage
has been done.

(V.O.):

6. CUTAWAY: MILITARY HELI'S.

Helicopter surveillance of the area
has been prevented by ground
artillery, but officials estimate
more than 2000 guerrillas and an
untold variety of weapons are in the

7. CUTAWAY: BLOCKADE.

zone. Streets have been sealed off with abandoned vehicles and sandbags, and all intersections are protected by guerrilla snipers.

COMMANDER A:

For us, it has often seemed that everyone is against us. We are the poor, the homeless, the cast-offs. The system has become our enemy. But the system is made up of individuals. It can be hard to see exactly who our enemies are. So we simply assume that if someone's not with us, he must be against us. This is the way the system thinks, so why not us? Trust no one. All are enemies. If not armed ones, then ideological ones. We are the armed, visible manifestation of resistance to the accepted ideology. We are war's dirt. Like I said, we do the dirty work, and we do it even for those who are too blind to understand.

DARYLL BRUCE:

Is killing part of the work?

HARRY LUND: (V.O.):

8. CUTAWAY: DAVID BEING RUSHED FROM AMBULANCE INTO HOSPITAL.

There is only one known escapee at this time, David Varley of Brunswick Avenue, who is presently unconscious and in serious but stable condition. He has gunshot wounds and internal injuries and is in shock. Neither doctors nor military officials were able to

get much information from him
before he lapsed into unconsciousness.

(SYNC):

9. REPORTER: O/C.   Anti-terrorist officials say it will
be just a matter of time before
the guerrillas' ammunition and
supplies run out and the
neighbourhood can be
re-occupied by the municipal,
provincial and national military forces.

(V.O.):

10. MCU: MAJOR WILSON: O/C.   Major Ernest Wilson is in
charge of the troops.

COMMANDER A:

We do what needs to be done. Our survival
is at stake. It might be necessary to kill. War is about death. And
war is about power. We fight because the power to determine
our own definition of freedom, our own freedom, has been taken
away, by the economic tug-of-war fought by those who control
wealth and seek to control more, and profit from it. They care
not for us. Yet we understand the irony, at least in the end. We
know that only occasionally is war really about freedom, and
even then it usually ends with repression. But if there is hope,
we must fight. The way it is now, one man's freedom is another
man's prison. One man's wealth is poverty for hundreds, thousands.

HARRY LUND: (SYNC):

11. REPORTER: O/C.   Major Wilson, what steps are being

taken to help the people who are

prisoners in their own

neighbourhood?

12. MAJOR WILSON: O/C. MAJOR WILSON: (SYNC):

A buffer zone one-quarter mile wide

has been established by our soldiers,

and access is denied to all but military

personnel. Residents evacuated

from the buffer zone are being

housed in hotels and schools or

with friends and neighbours.

We've been unable to free any

resident hostages, but we

expect shortly to establish

contact with the guerrillas.

13. REPORTER: O/C.   REPORTER: (SYNC):

What will be your strategy?

At every round, a nurse checks in on patient Varley, taking readings from his monitoring equipment. A military information specialist, sharing a round-the-clock watch, sits at the foot of the bed, continuously running a tape recorder, ready to question and take notes if David Varley becomes coherent.

COMMANDER A:

This is why I speak to you, to explain our

tactics. Yes, we attack neighbourhoods, citizens. For the system is everywhere. But we are only after the traitors, those who exploit us, those who hate us, and those who ignore us. Most of my comrades will not talk to you this way, will not talk to you at all. They trust no one but themselves. Not even the man next to them. I am speaking to you because you need to know all sides of the story.

MAJOR: (SYNC):

14. MAJOR WILSON: O/C. That's classified information, but we are taking measures to return the Annex to our control. We will be negotiating with the rebels to free the children now in captivity.

HARRY LUND: (V.O.):
Will you have to give something in exchange for the children's freedom?

MAJOR: (SYNC):
I'm not at liberty to discuss that.

15. REPORTER: O/C. HARRY LUND: (SYNC):
Thank you, Major Wilson. We will bring you further developments from the Annex as they occur. Officials have informed us that no other area of the central city is endangered at this time.

DARYLL BRUCE:
Speaking of citizens, innocent ones, what do you feel for your victims, like David Varley, the escaped

resident of the Annex? His wife and children also may be innocent victims of your attack.

COMMANDER A:

I do not know this man. I do not know his family. They are victims, you say? They were innocent? Only very young children are innocent.

DARYLL BRUCE:

The Varleys have two children, Bobby and Jennifer. They are missing and presumed in danger, if not injured or dead.

COMMANDER A:

This is unfortunate, but unavoidable. This is war.

16. HARRY LUND: O/C. HARRY LUND: (SYNC):
Business carries on in most parts of
downtown as usual, though some public
transit has been suspended. There has
been no change since last month in
the status of the occupied
suburban neighbourhoods,
Markland Woods and Military
Trail. We are following these stories and
will report as the stories break.

17. HEAD & SHOULDERS
ROBINSON. STUDIO. NOLAND ROBINSON: (SYNC):
Now, news on the lighter side...

COMMANDER A:

Our victims are victims of their own stupidity, their own refusal to see the truth. At the least, they are passively complicit; at the most, actively so. In this time, those who live in tranquillity are few, and are isolated from reality. We bring war to their doorsteps. This is our job. To bring the reality of the rest of the world into their living rooms. To shock them with the truth. To end their delusion.

DARYLL BRUCE:

Then you feel that you, and your soldiers, are messengers?

COMMANDER A:

No, the guerrilla is not the messenger. He is the message. He is the already dispossessed. He is you, if you could only see. But now he is a soldier. He has been given permission to fight. As a soldier, you do what you have to do to stay alive. That is all. Your life is a short life. You simply try to make your enemy's end sooner than your own.

David Varley lies in an alien world. A sterile, white, wired world. A room where he stares fixedly up to a bright light in the ceiling. Tubes enter his body from gurgling and pumping machines. Occasionally, he rolls his head from side to side, for minutes at a time. His shoulders, arms, hips and legs are pressed to the bed, held by restraining straps. His lips stay drawn tight across his teeth. White-uniformed attendants come regularly to his bed to check the equipment. They often stop at the edge of the bed, and speak. He does not respond. The built-in television has been removed from its bracket over his bed, because the news is often about him, and if he understood, he might find the images disturbing.

THE LEAK

COPY

Case	: Security violation 5197.
Item	: Personal diary fragment.
	(Attached - DOCUMENT A)
Location	: Bomb blast site #238. Forest district 11648.
Facility	: Underground. Built into lakeside elevation.
	Believed to be agent lair. Unregistered.
Condition	: Demolished.
Mode	: Plastic explosives. No other forensic evidence.
	Uncertain whether the site was infiltrated
	or self-destructed.
Documents	: As attached. No other documents.
Personnel	: One. Affiliation uncertain. Probably a Bureau
	operative, or double agent.
Circumstance	: Personality breakdown. Possible code violation.
Status	: No body found. Corpse removed or agent at large.
Security	: High risk.

DOCUMENT A

May 2.

I'm getting weaker. Body breaking down. Losing confidence in my mind's ability to hold.

Outside my window a spruce forest forms a thick shady curtain. Gaps here and there in the green let me see the shimmer of sun on the lake. I am walled in.

In a building with false walls and solid ones, all walls are suspected of containing secret passages.

May 3.

Someone has been assassinated. A cover-up is in effect. I am investigating. More to follow.

My official diary is sent to the Department as required. I keep two journals. This one is for you and you alone. You are MOST important to me. I see you in my mind's eye whenever I write this. I speak directly to you.

There will be no action here. No suspense. Just my exhausted, tiresome voice telling you what seems important through my isolated view. It's been sixteen weeks since I've seen another human.

I'm beginning to doubt the validity of the information I've been getting. It's not that I can't tell fact from fiction, because this distinction is immaterial, but rather that I'm growing suspicious of what's behind the data, of the reasons for the existence of certain fabrications. Is it possible that someone has penetrated the network? That one of my departed colleagues is an informer? Regardless, I continue to work analyzing data. I am the fitter in this puzzle with many pieces.

Dazzling reflections from the lake ignite for a few minutes each day when the angle of the sun is right. The glitter explodes into my dark cell. Otherwise, little light gets through the slit window. My eyes drink in what they can, but mostly I'm attuned to the glow of the screen, the darkness of night.

My fingers move on the keyboard, cast in a green patina that makes them seem ancient, skeletal. I am certain that they move slower now, with diminishing agility. My skin has become coarser, the pores more pronounced.

Meanwhile, I assemble the puzzle. I must understand the context in which the information I have found, or already know, will make an impact. Who might benefit and who might suffer? This must be clear when I synthesize the data into an official document.

May 4.

Cabin fever hit me last week, so I've started going outside at night. I douse the candles and lamps, suit up in my stealth uniform, complete with face-black, and slip out. I can breathe there, outside my camouflaged bunker. I love to feel the night air on my skin. To feel space around me. This contradicts orders, but here I'm in charge.

When I'm outside it is as if no one has been killed. But inside I cannot forget. The incident has been suppressed, and in official channels the death was labelled inconsequential. The Victim— V— has no formal status. No identity has been released.

I apologize to you; what follows may seem complex, but I'll try to be clear. This is information warfare. What I tell you is the truth despite what else you may hear.

The Target— T— was the intended victim. This has not been acknowledged. On the other hand, unofficial sources have confirmed that a murder has been reported, and that V, the Victim, was a person associated with T, though the connection is not clear. Apparently T was present at the time of the (non)assassination. This would in part explain the mistake.

If any version of this is finally presented as official, it may be by the one source that can lie without reproach. Or it may be the version that can be glossed over and forgotten most easily.

The death is affecting things, yet few know what has changed. Most wouldn't care. It is just information.

May 5.

Haven't been eating properly, though well-stocked with supplies.

Bored with cooking. My body has no desire for food. Can't hold much in, anyway.

Body not co-operating. Has turned against me. Now I'm even a danger to myself.

At night, I walk easily in the forest, though some parts are dense and deeply dark. My night vision has improved with practice and now I am able to discern shapes and even details of vegetation. I can identify species— fern and low bush cranberry, whatever— and I can spot animals scurrying through the brush. We have darkness in common, we nocturnal creatures.

Yet the story we live in the broad light of day remains without definition and shape, its closure hidden from us. Characters are incomplete and plot is based on details filtered through the labyrinths of our own minds, or through networks of the information machine. The story is manipulated by everyone who touches it. Do you remember the classroom game where a story is whispered from person to person and the end version is compared with the original? The results are considerably changed and usually funny. We prefer laughter to truth.

My mirror startled me this morning. When I looked in the glass I didn't recognize the face staring back. Bug-eyed, unshaven, muck caked in the corners of his mouth. I scrubbed with cold water and a coarse cloth. The stranger remained. Russet-faced, cleaner, but unfamiliar.

The manipulators, the data transformers, the programmers of the machine all have their hands in the story. Politicians, advisors, reporters, speculators, academics, editors, clergy, directors, spin doctors, agents like me. All kinds of anglers with access to the channels. Fabrication is easy for those with greater access. They can clog the networks or hide the goods. In North America every day, more than twenty-seven-thousand documents are labelled SE-CRET and removed from circulation. Information disappears. What's left over? The more powerful you are, the more channels you can manipulate by jamming or removal. And people believe what the channels give them, because they're too overwhelmed to examine what lies between the lines, or what's missing. Or they can't get far enough back to look at the big pattern. Many prefer to be receivers.

For the System, memory is most helpful when it fails. Human history lives on the plane of fiction. The truth dwells in the cave of the forgotten, in the pool of the invisible.

May 6.

May 7.

Yesterday— the fever— burning me up. Vomiting. Nothing left inside. Or outside.

No single person or agency is in charge. Factions are engaged in a soft war. Yet it is not without casualties. Of course this reality is never stated outright. The true power matrix prefers low or no visibility, and false attribution. But I'm sure you know this.

I have been assigned the task of finding the bottom line of the assassination attempt. The Bureau does not know that I was an operative in the plot. I am investigating something I know all about, yet I must go through the motions of finding out what happened, and in fact arrive at untruth as a result.

This is not as easy as it might seem, because everything I do or say, every source, every conclusion, must be documented. I thought I knew all the facts, yet my research is turning up information that surprises me. You see, even I am not above naïveté.

I've been calling up mug shots of people I'm investigating. The face of power is so often benign, so bland. T looks fresh, healthy, seems to improve in appearance with power, no matter the intrigues that circle him. Why then do I, caught in the same intrigues, though in another orbit, deteriorate, while he thrives?

Yes, I have called up my own visage. The picture they're transmitting is years out of date. This indicates a certain success. I'm becoming untraceable. I can't be recognized. Between the plastic surgeries, ageing, and my current sickness...

I have wanted to call up your image. I resist though, in case my transactions are ever traced. I do not wish to implicate you. But I long for contact, despite the training. I must be burnt out, losing my edge. The will to maintain my canny guard, my radar, is weakening. But I think of you. Your skin. The scent of you. Your eyes. To have the image of your face would be to have part of you here with me. Transmitted into my life by our wondrous technology. Have no fear. I will not jeopardize you. I will call up any image but yours. I will rely on memory.

May 8.

I've seen foxes, porcupines, lots of rabbits, skunks and racoons. Owls are easy to spot because their eyes shine as if with their own light. I'm the only human around, I think, yet I am no blessing to these animals. They are pure, they survive by being specialized. They know what they need to know, and they use their knowledge intensely.

We gather any information that can be quantified. In the name of knowledge we amass data, but we're no better off. Such superfluous detail is irrelevant to the animals, yet in our hands it kills them. We are the bizarre ones.

I will have to be careful with the information I release. Careful not to reveal what I know, unless it is to my advantage. I am in danger. Someone knows that I know too much. I am in violation of my oath. Everyone violates some oath.

Everyone inside and outside the organization with a guilty conscience or with something to protect, fears discovery. My research is secret, yet everyone knows that investigation of everything is continuous. They could find themselves exposed or convicted. Everyone has dirty laundry. How's yours? I hope that those with the dirtiest laundry remain silent, or that fear immobilizes them.

Being far away has advantages. And disadvantages. I feel safe, but unsafe. This takes its toll.

I've stopped reading for relaxation. I spend so much time reading and rereading data every day. No longer any pleasure in the flow of words from someone else's imagination. I write to you. It lets me see my words, my thoughts, outside me. I can trust them, can't I? Can you?

May 9.

At dawn, as I came in after walking last night, a bird flew through the open door. I didn't realize this right away, although I had sensed a subtle movement that I thought was my shadow. It was a bluebird, a stunning shade of turquoise blue, with a bit of rust and grey. Trapped inside, the bird panicked, flew frantically to the walls, the window slits, to no avail. It couldn't find the door. Finally it settled, was quiet, then began making soft churring sounds. I put out some berries. It eats them when I'm not nearby. Otherwise, it perches in a corner on the ceiling beam and sometimes it hides. I've been leaving the door open, contrary to regulations (again!).

Still vomiting. Throat is scraped raw and the acid erodes my teeth enamel. Stomach cramps like it's caught in a vice. Am I being poisoned?

I work at the terminal in a small room jammed with files. My tolerance for long hours at the screen has been reduced. My fingers weaken and my eyes blur and sting. Yesterday my access to outside data banks was interrupted. Have I been sabotaged, or are there technical problems? I know you're familiar with the most advanced systems. What would you suspect? Otherwise, I gather and think, using these tools, my intuition, and the logic of my humble brain, piecing together what I know and what I find out. I choose to reveal or to withhold. I have dug far beyond the scope of my assignment. I must be extremely careful to avoid detection. If a bluebird can find me...

May 10.

Something important:

I was called into a clandestine meeting ten months ago. There was only the Chairman and I. The rest participated by teleconference. The words used were circumspect and guarded. We all understood what was being talked about. There were seven of us. Code names applied. Four were assigned to the Battery Unit, two for the hit, and two for cover. I was a cover. The other three— called Facelift— would move into the structure later, at the time of the changes.

Battery Unit dropped by helicopter onto the roof after midnight. Concorde Building. We lowered ourselves on lines down the elevator shaft to floor twelve. Two of us stayed in the shaft, dropping to eleven; two took the stairwell. We waited, then popped the shaft doors on eleven, drawing both security guards. We were above the doors, out of sight. Our colleagues rattled the stairwell door. The guards turned and we roped them backwards into the shaft, let them go. The wind whistled. Their bodies cludded to the bottom like bundles of newspapers.

We burst into the meeting room two at a time. Somebody snuffed the lights. Dark scurry. Gun blasts. Two marksmen fired blind from memory's glimpse and from intelligence briefings. Ten seconds later, as planned, we pulled out. All four clambering up the stairwell. I trailed for cover, stopped to listen at every other landing. No one in pursuit. At the roof, the wind hit me like needles. I smashed my shins, stumbling on the transom. Helicopter blades diced the starlight, clattered my bones. In, up, gone. Air chafed our gaping mouths, burned our heaving chests.

May 11.

I get nervous when I hear power boats on the lake. I don't go to the shore, even at night. There may be observation posts nearby, or other surveillance. I long to dip my hands in the water, skip a stone across the waves, or walk along the water's edge. The face-black has given me a rash. Flies are getting in.

I report by mail, sending a package every week to a safe contact in the city. Usual security procedures— an envelope inside another inside another and so on. The package makes its way through several screens who strip off the outside envelope, burn it, then forward the next envelope. No return addresses. Seems antiquated in these electronic times, but it is, as you know, the traditional method. I also file e-logs. You can't locate me. No one can. Neither my superiors, nor my detractors. The matrix is not listed and no one, not even the telecommunications corporation, has the number. Information transfers are done through a series of renegade networks to avoid detection. I am shielded by invisible walls. I am hidden and exposed at the same time. Absent and present. But as I've said, the System is deteriorating.

And so is mine. My eyebrows falling out. Do you know this condition? Does it have a name? I first noticed the errant hairs on my keyboard, then clinging to my finger tips when I'd wipe my brow. How many features can a face lose and still remain a face?

May 12.

The bluebird disappeared today, the third day of our companionship. I miss the distraction, the evidence of another life besides my own. I grew fond of the fellow, though I knew he wasn't mine to keep.

You must figure out why I am telling you all this. And you must determine whether I am speaking the truth or not, whether I have something to gain by giving you false information. I'm stating this outright, because I know that no amount of assurance will convince you absolutely to trust this document. It could even be forged.

Soon you will begin hearing things through the usual networks, public and clandestine, and the details will fall into place. You may be the only one with the chart to fit the pieces into. This puts you in a powerful but vulnerable position.

You will need to know the following. We eliminated the wrong target. We all escaped and resumed normal duties, and, as far as we know, we remain above suspicion. Theories have been advanced, but none of them have included even one of our team. I have found out that V was a secret advisor to T. That's why he was in the room. By our mistake, we have made an impact, albeit at a subtler level, but not without significance. T remains in his position, and is silent on the matter.

How can an anonymous, non-existent body— mine— be filled in its very tissue with such toxicity, such weakness?

You are the only recipient of this information. Do not release it, if at all, until I'm standing in a room with you and give approval. In such a case, I will use the words Bluebird Report. Otherwise, reveal nothing until you are certain of my death. They are not above faking an obituary. Wait until you've seen the body. Realize that you may be at risk. Information is dangerous. Perhaps you should never have read this. On the other hand, all this may become lost in the flood of facts and fictions, another incomprehensible bit in a large unfathomable puzzle. Well, you and I will know one thread of truth, and you will know even more.

The telephone rang this morning.

May 13.

The bluebird reappeared, with a mate, who is building a nest on the beam in the corner. They must feel safe. I call them Blue and Beulah. My generosity with fruit and berries may result in living day and night with the door open and the constant chirping cries of hungry bluebird chicks. Company.

Sick again. Went walking nonetheless. Overcome by strange clarity borne of weakness and fever. Astounding. No light in overcast night sky. The woods deep deep black, eerie, still.

The whole story may never be known. I trust you to never acknowledge our contact, even in the above-mentioned situations. Such an admission would be unfortunate, worse for you and for others than for me.

Have worked hard. Dedication to duty cannot be questioned. Of course, certain factions will discredit me. What is achieved? Far more to convey. For now I send you this much. First thing tomorrow.

Remember the walls.

END OF COPY

Hammond at the Bluenote

Dear Karl,

Wind gusts knifed blades of cold air through my coat flaps, up my sleeves, and jabbed dust motes into my eyes. Lisa and I were on our way to the Bluenote for John Hammond's one-night-only gig before he moved on to Saskatoon. Maybe that unexpected wind was a premonition, but I didn't know it. The burly doorman insisted we check our coats. I felt like we were in New York City, where another practice lets them take you for another dollar. I protested. He insisted. My mind searched for the logic of compulsory coat checking. Maybe people don't fight when their coats are checked. Perhaps coats slung over the backs of chairs droop onto the floor creating hazards for waiters. We checked our coats. I even tipped the attendant, a slim fellow in a loose-fitting tie-dyed shirt and a droop-down moustache, like a character stuck in the sixties.

We searched the long narrow room for a good vantage point, and crammed into a table dead centre about twenty feet from the stage. People were drinking beer and chatting quietly, greeting friends and ordering drinks, waiting for the show. A bouffant-blonde waitress in a tight leather skirt paused to take our order. This could have been a blues bar in any city in North America, any white middle-class city, that is. Square arborite tables with chrome legs, black vinyl chairs, a stand-up bar to the right, stage at the back end, and behind that, the washrooms, so you could always grab a peek backstage on your way to the can.

The small stage glowed faint red in the subtle wash of dimmed spotlights. A stool sat empty behind two microphones, one at the height for a guitar, and one for voice. A waiter passed with a tray full of beer glasses held on his upturned left palm, level with his shoulders. Without really looking I absorbed his impression as he walked by. I turned to speak to Lisa. Suddenly his image registered. I blinked and looked again, caught the waiter's back disappearing around the corner toward the bar. *Karl, what are you doing here,* I thought, *in a bar, serving drinks, fifteen-hundred miles from Toronto?*

He wasn't an exact replica, but it was you, or some aspect of you. Did you know you were doing this? I mean, does the other you know? The publisher of the avant-garde... that you. Does that one know that his other is working a blues bar?

I wrote my impressions on the menu 'Specials' insert. I'll copy them here so you can see my thoughts exactly as they came to me that night.

He flickers through the room, carrying a full tray. He has darting eyes, a tight jaw. He's you, but he's different. His walk is quicker, less athletic. I wonder if he reads. He looks like he might read Nabokov, but not Burroughs, and I'm sure he's never heard of your heroes, Joseph Beuys or John Cage, or even Dave McFadden.

I wonder now how I could have made those assumptions. But we often do this, don't we? Make assumptions about people simply on the strength of a glance? I can imagine him doing karate, like you, and I can see you slinging beer. But the edges are different. Maybe that's it. You're both at edges, but on different sides of them. He might be someone who leaves work later and does something dangerous. Drugs maybe, or sado-sex, brawling in a booze can, or using weapons.

He's wearing black pants and a white shirt, with a silver change dispenser on his belt. You wear black and white, too. He's shorter than you, and slighter, more wiry, and moves more quickly, like a water spider.

I felt like asking him if he'd ever heard of Mr. Bedoya, or if he was familiar with the vocabulary of torture. But I was afraid he'd take it the wrong way— I mean, I didn't think he would have known the literary connection, but then, how many do— read, I mean— to see things through the eyes of words?

Lisa interrupted me at this point to ask what I was doing. I told her and she laughed, seeming to understand, though she's never met you. I pointed him out to her. She nodded, then studied him till he passed out of sight. She said he didn't look like a writer, but couldn't say why. I wonder if she'd think you look like a writer. What do we look like, anyway?

He's just behind me now, on the other side of a standing bar. Someone slaps him on the shoulder. He backs away with that stiff-legged jousting move that guys have with each other in locker rooms, moving to avoid the flicking towel without losing composure. He pops a cigarette package from his shirt pocket. Lights up with his lips drawn tight, bottom lip forcing the cigarette to a slight upward angle, hands sheltering the flame. He exhales aggressively. The slapping switches to a friendly posturing, jibing, and strutting. I've never seen you do this, but I can imagine it.

I began to wonder if I was just making all this up. You know, building a fiction around nothing, exercising my imagination. Lisa told me to go on note-taking, that if nothing else, there might be an idea for a story in all this. She's practical.

I'm concerned, finding this other you running around, using up energy. This can't be good for you. Where's that energy coming from? It's got to be from your reserve. Are you feeling tired lately? If you are whole this other shouldn't be loose. It's a sign to me that all is not well. That there's some kind of dissociation going on with you. Is that right? I don't mean to stir things up, but this is how it feels to me. Our doubles get away, then there's trouble. When you're feeling low on energy, maybe it's because there's another one of you out there, draining you, appearing in a place like a bar, a place that he can easily disappear from when you get more unified. Or maybe he changes into some other other, and gets fuel from a new source. Or maybe we ourselves are others.

In his presence that night everything I thought and wrote down made complete sense. Lisa insists that all this double stuff is just coincidence, that with so many people in the world, some are bound to resemble others. She suggests that you and he may be distant relatives. That could be. Do you have any cousins here? Lisa says she feels like she's met you now. Here's my final note.

The blonde must be on a break, because he approaches our table to take our order for a second round. When he brings the drinks, I ask him his name, say he looks like someone I know. He says he's Jerry Carleton. I ask him if he has any relatives back east. His dark steely eyes tell me he doesn't want any more questions. He sets our beers down, scoops up our money and moves off without another word.

John Hammond hunched over his guitar on the club's small stage.

The crowd was enthusiastic and must have spurred him on with their cheers and applause, because he played an extra-long last set. He ended with a version of Robert Johnson's *Preachin' Blues* that blew the place apart. Writhing and twisting with the music, light glinting off his wailing old National guitar. Finger slide on his left hand riding up and down the neck. Legs twitching. Voice soaring and growling. Did you hear John Hammond music in your head that night— Monday, the 2nd? That would be proof.

It took us a while to get to the coat-check room, with all the people trying to shuffle out at the same time. As I was helping Lisa slip her coat on, a scuffle broke out in the middle of the bar. The place went silent. It was Jerry and a stringy-looking dude with glassy eyes who looked like he was on uppers. Everybody backed away. Jerry was crouched in a karate position. The dude had a knife. Its blade moved about two feet from Jerry's nose. I broke through the crowd at the same time as the club bouncer. We moved toward the two of them. Our approach diverted Jerry, and Stringy lunged at him. The bouncer and I were on the guy a second too late. Jerry'd taken the knife in the side.

He'd looked just like you in that karate position. That was what snapped me. I thought it was you. You know me, I don't usually jump into barroom brawls. But I had to help, for your sake. Lisa gave me hell later for getting into something that didn't concern me, for letting my crazy imagination run away with me. I don't think she understood. Mind you, I don't either. I mean, you're there and I'm here, and just because someone looks like you... Did you feel any pain that night, in your side? Did you fight? Is everything okay?

The bloodstain on Jerry's shirt was large, just below his left armpit. They rushed him to the hospital.

It was a long time before we got out of the Bluenote that night. Seems Stringy had refused to pay his bar bill and pulled a knife on Jerry. The police questioned me and took a statement, along with my name and address, so I guess I'll hear more about this.

I called the club the next day and they told me that the blade had cut close to his lung, so he'd gone into intensive care overnight, and then to the recovery ward, where he must be now. I don't know when I'll run into him again, except maybe in court. You have never met him (can I assume that?), so all this may not mean very much. I'm going to mail a copy of your book to him at the hospital. Maybe that'll close some kind of gap between you two. Anyway, I hope you both keep out of trouble.

Did you think of me that night? Were you drinking beer? Do me a favour: don't take a job in a bar. Just keep writing stories and publishing your magazine. What are your stories about these days? Do you suppose I'm off the deep end? Let me know... about everything.

It was warmer when we got outside. The wind was still up, but refreshing; it cleared my head. Lisa and I hugged together as we walked home. Still, I began to shiver when I realized what had actually happened. It scared me, because I had simply gone with Lisa to see John Hammond, and we ended up in somebody else's story.

Regards,
Danny

TIE - BURNER

orange fire clusters punctuate the darkness at regular intervals in a line receding to a hidden horizon. the size of each pyre shrinks proportionately in the perspective of distance, scars branding deep into night's black skin.

i have read of ancient fire rituals. of prayer. of sacrifice. of immolation. of fire's wrath. of the flames of passion. of the atomic fire-wind that sucks all into its maw. i have seen animal flesh on the spit dripping fat into flame. i have heard of ordinary humans who blaze into sainthood.

rails gleam metallic in the amber light. fumes of gasoline nauseate with a scent never familiar enough to slip from notice. an intruder in its alliaceous family. an infiltrator that fills my nostrils, my sinuses, my throat. gasoline and diesel. diesel that fuels my small jigger car and gasoline from the can i carry. these smells cling to me. in the cramped jigger the small hard seat and stick throttle are my closest travelling companions. a chain-saw rides on the floor next to me.

i live with fire. commit burial by flame. i am the high priest of ritual. my torrid beacons fester in the night. i am the tie-burner.

i work alone. i've been out of the main depot four days, travelling east on the south link line. by day, to take advantage of the light, i slice and pile the old ties left by track crews. by night i soak the piles in gasoline and set them ablaze. on this section there's a pile every fifty feet. it's repetitive work, but not easy. i'm strong and careful. i know what i'm doing. i like the rhythm. the day's beat: haul/cut/pile/move-on/haul/cut/pile/move-on. the night beat: soak/ignite/ride/soak/ignite/ride/soak/ignite/ride.

through the day i work my way east, cutting and piling. in the late afternoon i start igniting where i finish cutting and work my way back west, setting fires.

lighting a fire is a spiritual act. a transformation of matter. i baptize the severed tie-corpses with gasoline. i attend as the fluid seeps in. i regard the change in the wood's surface as it seems to dry like a blotter. i turn away. with my back to the pile i ignite my torch. holding the fire at arm's length, i turn. it cuts a half circle in the night. i reach down. touch flame to wood. flare. stand close as i dare. revel in the burst of heat. contemplate the flame's race through the ties. pile becomes pyre. i stay close until the heat pushes me back.

when they're all lit, i turn east again, checking each fire to make sure it's not spreading off rail land. if it is, i scatter the timbers, douse with earth.

at the end of a night i sit gazing at the last flames. i can stare into a burning tie-pile for a long time. into its white-hot heart. fire speaks with the staccato fricative of evil. or the holy rustle of angels. or the tormented cries of shackled spirits. all the crumbling echoes of my own memory.

i light a cigarette, this too a ritual. a ration of one each day. i stare
into the blaze. drag on the cigarette. feel the fire on me. in me.

an old face with bright eyes appears. tries to speak to me from the
jabbing flame. syllables lost in the crackle and spit.

      fades

          slowly

              away

fire burns low

          a breeze builds

              a howl

a blast of wind knocks me over. embers explode. leap like shooting
stars. like bullets. into the grass. fire tears through dry brush. surrounds
me. i stumble up the embankment to the track. grab my shovel from
the jigger. beat at flames. scoop spades full of earth on them. fires
extinguish then pop back to life. sweat pours down my brow. floods
my eyes. soaks through my thick shirt. dig / beat / run / beat/beat
/ dig / run. this fire will not be stopped. laps up around the jigger.
i dig under the fire. try to push it down the slope. parts of the car
are burning. someone seems to be laughing. or calling. my coveralls
ignite. i throw myself to the ground. roll and beat / roll and beat.
flash. the car explodes. concussive. chunks of flaming metal hurl over
my head. hissing. thudding into the ground all around me.

when it is calm i open my eyes, raise my head. twisted sizzling wheels lie where the handcar had been... a stinging in my flesh...

...silence...

...wet on my face. on my hands...

thunder.

rain. rain.

in no time the land darkens as all fire drowns in the downpour. smell of smoke and smouldering ash hovers close to the ground. i am soaked through to my skin. i must find wood that isn't wet. start a fire to dry out.

i move into the night. i am blackened like the sky, like the charred grass. i follow the track. i seek fire. i walk. become nearly invisible. stumble occasionally against a raised tie. begin to weary.

those faces. the voices. i know them. i know. them.

after some time i come upon a tie-pile still glowing deep in its centre. i blow gently into its fiery heart, nudge a few logs carefully. life returns in flames. i move to the next pile. drag a dry tie back to the burning one. repeat. repeat. the fire builds. flames leap. i sit. patiently fanning. stoking. renewing fire's spirit. tongues of flame flicker before my eyes.

i fall to my knees before the blaze. bow my head.

a voice speaks: "i am lost. you are lost. give me your hand."

i put my hand in the fire. there is no pain. warmth fills my whole body. i move closer.

"you must not turn away."

my hand is released. i bring it to my eyes. it is not marked. i lower my hand.

logs collapse inward. the fire flares orange and blue. a baby floats in the flames. crying. crying. tiny thin arms flailing against the licking flame. blue flame. cold flame. chills his skin. face distorts with wailing. legs trying to kick free. arms beating for warmth. alone. so close to heat. so cold. so alone.

a voice calls. the old man's face hovers above the heat. i know this face. i stand. peer into the smoke. the baby's cries are inside me now. i spread my arms. the fire is all around me.

LURES

Calvin sits in the living room in the brown tweed chair. On the wall behind him hangs an oceanscape, waves spraying over rocks in a turbulent sea, set off by a seashell-encrusted frame. In front of him and drawing his stare is a television. The screen is dark, the room silent.

The door latch clicks and Calvin turns his gaze to meet his visitor.

"Come right in. Glad to see you found your way." He rises from the chair. "I just shut the TV off. Soaps and talks. Can't stand them after a while. Rather watch bad hockey than that stuff. Game tonight should be good... So, you're here to see the merchandise." Calvin's gesture sweeps the living room. "It's all for sale. In the kitchen and other rooms, too. Have a look. Ask me about anything, rugs, furniture, appliances, pictures. Time to lighten my load." He hikes his pants up by the belt, stands ready to advise, ready to play the role of the salesman.

"Coffee?" he says, turning to walk, stiff-legged, into the kitchen. A microwave oven stands on the counter beside the toaster-oven, and beside that, a toaster, and a bread box with the door open. Empty. He reaches for the handle on the fridge.

"I keep the coffee in the freezer to keep it fresh. Bread, too. Fridge is for sale, but you'd have to wait. It'll be last to go."

An egg-shaped device is attached to the outside of the door, beside the automatic ice dispenser. Calvin sets the coffee can on the counter; the refrigerator door closes beside him under its own momentum. Opening a cupboard drawer Calvin removes a hand-wind can opener. He gestures toward the green appliance attached to the counter wall.

"Electric one's broken. I'll throw it in with whatever you take, no charge. Maybe you can fix it."

After a few tries, Calvin pierces the can, releasing a hiss. He turns the opener around the lid. Rich coffee aroma fills the air. Using a cone-shaped plastic spoon, he measures six scoops of brown granules into a paper filter sitting in the plastic funnel. He flips this into place, fills a Pyrex measuring cup from the tap and pours the water into the Melitta chamber. He pours in four more cupfuls, then flicks the switch.

He leans his hip on the counter and turns toward the window. A small box sits on the sill. He presses its lever, and it emits a brief hum and pops a tooth-pick through a slot. He takes it and pokes at his teeth.

"Go ahead, look around. I'll leave you alone to think. I'll clean up here while the coffee's brewing." He lifts a plate of leftovers and scrapes the remains of noodles and bread crusts into the garburetor. With a throaty rumble, the mechanical digestive track gobbles up the refuse.

He moves toward the kitchen doorway, calls down the hall, "Me and the missus bought this garburetor with my sales bonus, our twentieth anniversary. Practical, she told me. Sanitary. The missus, she liked things clean. We were younger then, in our thirties, still in love. Seemed the right thing. Runs as good as the first day. Comes out easy and can be installed in any sink." Calvin shuts the machine off and reaches into a flowered cookie tin.

"I've got danishes to go with your coffee," he calls.

He slips two buns into the microwave, presses the timer and a soft whirr of the oven blurs out the sound of the coffee maker, its brown stream trickling into the pot.

"If you take the whole lot I'll give you a volume discount," he chuckles.

The flow of coffee from the funnel hesitates as the last drops sputter. Calvin lifts the pot. Stray drips sizzle on the element. He pours steaming coffee into two mugs, and pushes one along the counter, past the Vegomatic food dicer and electric carving knife.

"Good coffee. Black's the only way to drink it."

Ding. He opens the microwave door, hot-hands the danishes onto two separate plates. He passes one plate and lifts the other, taking the danish and biting in. He blows on his coffee while chewing. Takes a sip.

"Seen everything in the bedroom, then? Dresser's an antique, you know. Came over from the old country. Solid. There's your coffee. Be careful, the danish was nuked. My daughter Merna had the right idea when she took me to get that microwave at an Eaton's sale. Up till the end, Helen'd done all the cooking. I blew up a potato first time, but now I can even poach an egg in there. Never was able to do that on the normal stove. So, I'll be keeping the microwave. Speaking of eggs, ever seen one of these?"

He points to the egg shape on the fridge door.

"Egg-shell piercer. You know how boiling an egg always makes it crack? The pressure builds up inside when it's boiling, pushing out on the shell, till, poof! Well, this piercer, you see you push the end of the egg onto a little spike that pops out and punctures the egg. Then when the egg's boiling, the pressure build-up is released through the hole, and the shell doesn't crack. Brilliant invention! This one's stuck and the spike doesn't poke out. Kinda like us old gaffers. Heh, heh, heh."

Calvin moves back to the living room, crosses the mustard shag-pile wall-to-wall beneath his feet. He sits on the bench in front of the organ, presses the on button, and plays the first quick notes of "Old MacDonald," followed by a line of "Amazing Grace."

"They tell you that retirement can kill you, you need things to do, you have to develop interests. So I decided I'd play the organ. Found out you could play by following the numbers. The salesman had me believing I'd be playing Beethoven in six weeks. Turns out it wasn't that easy. I still sit down and finger out the odd tune from time to time, but I never got to the *Ninth Symphony*. Heh, heh. I was happy with a few Christmas carols, though. "Jingle Bells" and "O Come All Ye Faithful." Good thing to have at Christmas. You play any instruments? No. I bet you're a reader. I read lots, too."

He takes a sip, then sets the coffee cup next to a clock on a stand beside the organ.

"See this clock? Kinda looks antique. Art-deco-LED. they called it. Was a free gift for buying subscriptions to three magazines for a year. You've got to keep up with what's going on in the world, eh? So why not get a gift for it? Just because you're retired doesn't mean the mind goes into neutral. If you want the clock, I'll throw in a bunch of magazines, too."

He shuffles toward the tweed chair. Rests his hand on its back.

"This is my relaxin' chair. Does everything. Sits up, tilts back, foot rest, vibrator, gives a massage, keeps the blood circulating. Many's the time I've fallen asleep on it, became so relaxed I vibrated right to dreamland. Been using it regularly since the day I bought it, just after Helen's funeral. I guess I needed comforting. It's not for sale."

He slips into the chair. Flips the vibrator switch. The motor begins to hum. He picks up the TV remote control. Flicks on a snowy picture.

"I-interference from the ch-ch-air." His voice wobbles as the chair's vibrations pass through his body.

"C-c-an-n-n't-t d-do m-m-u-u-ch-ch a-a-b-b-ou-t-t-t i-i-t-t."

The TV hisses, the picture discernible but fuzzy.

"L-lookit-t that-t. A-a m-m-eal in a-a p-ou-ou-ch. Mus-st b-be w-what the a-astro-n-n-auts ate. J-j-ust p-po-p it i-in boil-ling w-wa-ater. G-g-ourmet stu-ff-fft-too. I-I don't hav-ve t-to lear-n-n to c-c-ook af-f-fter a-ll-ll. L-l-et's s-ee-ee if the n-n-ews is-s on, s-s-ee who's mess-ess-in' u-u-p-p th-th-ings today-y."

Channels blink past as he pushes the remote button. Click.

"I know that God is listening to your prayers," says a smooth-faced evangelist. Click.

The awkward bulk of a hippopotamus rises in slow motion from a river mud bath to the punting tune of tuba music.

Click.

"Trouble in Washington's black ghetto tonight," says an attractive news commentator through her bright make-up and perfectly coiffed hair. Click.

Calvin settles back, sets the control wand on the colonial coffee table beside a ceramic frog with a tiny plant growing out of its back, elfin figures peeking around toadstools, and a bulky ship's wheel ashtray. The television picture is still snowy, the hum of the vibrator steady. He switches the vibrating speed to low.

"Tha-at's a little better. Better picture too. Now h-here's modern shop-ping, the Sh-shopping Channel. Don't even have t-to leave home. I bought a whole set of fish-sh-ing lures last week. Haven't been fishing f-for years. Rod's-s gone missing. I h-h-ave to order one, soon, prob-ob-ably right off this sh-show... So don't l-l-et my ch-ch-atter keep you from looking ar-ar-ound. Most every-thing's for sale. D-don't be afraid to a-s-sk about anything, even-n if I said I was attached to it-t. It's all in g-g-ood shape, looked after. Needs a goo-oo-d h-home. These things'll give you p-p-leasure, comfort. I know their va-a-alue. But I can't really s-set a price, so-o-o make me an offer. Not on the chai-ai-r, the TV, the microw-w-ave, or the lur-ure-es though. D-d-on't even try. More coff-ff-ee?"

He pauses. The television light plays on his pale face.

"Yeah, real t-t-ime savers. Make m-me a reason-n-n-able offer."

Damn'd Hand

The meperidine must be wearing off. Hot pains shoot through my hand, radiate outside my flesh, multiply, then stab back in, hundreds of fiery pokers. I ask Nurse Bradshaw for something stronger, but she says that would be morphine, and it has bad side effects. No pill. No position on this hospital bed gives me relief.

~

"Eee-ee-ee-k," Ezz screams.

Jilly shouts, "Delbert, that's cruel."

I hold the finch right up where my sisters have to look, squeeze it tight in my hand so it can't budge, and pluck the feathers, one by one.

"Cheeeep-eeep," squeaks the finch.

"You'll go to hell, Delbert," says Jilly.

"Oowww-oooowwww," wails Ezz.

They can't stop watching. They peek, hide their eyes, peek again, their squeals cut the air, drowning out the screaky finch. Ezz's shrieks bug me. Shrill and whiney. Still it feels good to make her do it, and Jilly too, but she doesn't get hysterical. She just watches me with a cold stare. Same as she's done ever since she was born.

~

"You're lucky to have a hand to feel pain in," says Bradshaw, her freckled fingers jamming a needle in my forearm.

That's what the doctors have been telling me since I came here, after my work glove caught in the auger. I reached in to free a stone jammed in the auger's mouth and the blade turned, yanked my left arm in, and zip, sliced the back of my hand to the wrist. Just like that. I passed out, didn't even know what happened. Thanks to the wife, I didn't bleed to death. Apparently Betty rushed me and my smashed half-severed hand to the hospital in town; they did some treatment, then put me on a jet to Toronto. Next thing I know, I'm here, green room, strange bed, unfamiliar city out the window, a giant fire at the end of my left arm, the arm lying across my stomach.

I can't feel a connection between my brain and my fingers. That's probably good, since I'm not supposed to move anything anyway. Doctor Preece came by and explained what she'd done. A bandage made of my own skin. She wrapped the wound in a graft of skin lifted from my abdomen, but still attached, so the blood and fluids flow into the tissue while it takes. She even grafted two tendons and a nerve from my leg into my wrist. If she did the job right, and if my body co-operates, the wound will heal, the nerve and tendons will start to mesh. She'll sever the graft from my abdomen, sew the flap of skin to my arm, the skin will take and my hand will be almost good as new. She said it was a team effort in the operating room, not just her alone. "Now you're part of the team," she said. I don't know about that. But I'm in no position to argue. And I got to tip my hat to her and her modern medicine!

~

I drop the naked bird on the ground. It doesn't move. Jilly and Ezz are silent. Wind swishes the trees. Sometimes the birds try to run, sometimes they flap their naked wings. This one just lies there until I pick it up again. Holding this bird, its last trembling bit of life cupped in my palm, I feel hot and powerful. I take its tiny head between my fingers. The girls scream. I twist its neck, and toss it into the caragana bush. Scratch and thump in the branches and it's all over. Ezz and Jilly stop shrieking. Everything stops but Jilly's stare and the hum of cicadas. Louder, louder, louder. The heat makes me dizzy.

~

Nurse Bradshaw said, "Think about pleasant things. This will help ease the pain. It's a trick called waking imagined analgesia."

She wrote that down for me. Fancy words for mind over matter. Doesn't work too well, no matter what you call it. I'd take the morphine. So anyway, I'm thinking up hand jokes. I'd be laughing if I wasn't so afraid I'd pop a stitch. Imagine shaking hands with a guy with a hand coming out of his belly button. Ha! Betty'll find me fun to dance with. I'll tickle her fancy. Heh-heh! But Betty and I don't dance now. I guess you could say we're not in step. Anyway, I'm working on thinking away my pain.

~

"She's a looker," the grade ten guys say, "that Betty Robertson."

I used to call her Barfy Betty because she threw up twice one day in grade one. She gave me a pain in public school when she sat in front of me because of the alphabet, and always gave the right answers. But since the last week of high school, this summer, something about her has me hanging around, in town at the DQ, or out on the road by her farm.

I follow the edge of the field and approach the dugout. I hear splashing, singing. So I sneak up. She's skinny-dipping, her pale flesh shining like a trout's belly in the murky water. I take out my slingshot and fire a pebble into the water beside her. Then another.

"I know you're there, Delbert. Come out of the bushes. I'm not going to get out of this water until I know you're not watching."

"Hi, Betty," I say, stepping to the edge.

"Turn away," she tells me.

I obey. Behind me the water sloshes as she steps out. I imagine her naked body gleaming in twilight.

"You can turn around now."

Dressed in shorts and a halter top, she walks toward me, around the edge of the dugout. Drips of water run from her red hair onto her shoulders. And onto her halter making the fabric stick against her breasts. I break out in a sweat. Have to put my hand in my pocket, grab myself so she doesn't see my bulge. I'd rather use my hands on her.

~

"Delbert," my Mom calls, approaching my hideout in the caragana. "I know you're here."

I hesitate, then step out of my branched cave. In Mom's round, usually happy face, her eyes are dark and burning, her forehead wrinkled, her mouth set. She carries a spade and a shoe-box.

"Turn around and take down your pants," she says. "Bend forward and hold onto that tree."

"What for?"

"The sooner you obey, the sooner you'll know."

I turn, dig my fingers into the sharp bark. Smack!

"One for the finch." Right on my naked rear with her bare hand. Smack!

"One for the chipping sparrow."

"One for the red-winged blackbird." Smack!

"For the warbler." Smack!

Smack! "For the wren." Smack!

"For the barn swallow."

Smack! "For the chickadee."

Smack! Smack!

"For all the rest." Smack. "Now turn around and look at me."

I turn. She's rubbing the palm of her hand with her fingers.

"Find the finch's body and give it a proper burial. You're eight. It's time you learned that killing is unkind, mischief has consequences, cruelty and murder are the devil's work. You've got a pact with the demons, don't you, Delbert? Here's the spade. Put the bird in this box, and before you close it, look at the bird and tell it you're sorry, dig a hole, and bury it. Then come and get me to show me the grave."

She turns toward the house.

I dig and dig, at the edge of the bush, my behind stinging. I hunt in the bushes, reach in for the finch. A branch spears into my shoulder.

"Fuck!" I've never said that before. "Fuck." I pick up the bird, so small, a slip of nothing, a nothing that makes me sore. Nothing I deserve. I hold it. I cannot speak to it. I close my fingers over it, my dirty nails. I pretend it's just a stone.

"I'm sorry."

I squeeze and squeeze.

"I hate you, Jilly!"

Squeeze until I feel wet mush, and green and crimson liquid seeps between my fisted fingers.

"Hate you, fuckin' Jilly!"

~

My Doc says this is a new procedure. If she pulls this one off, or should I say, sticks this one on, I'll be amazed. She won't give me odds on my chances.

"What happens if the nerves and tissues don't take," I ask.

"You might lose a digit or two."

That's what she calls them, digits. Don't sound too important that way.

"If that happens, you might still have some function in the remaining fingers, if you're lucky. At worst, you could lose the hand, but I don't think that'll be the case."

"I'm worried about my work on the farm, about being an invalid, about gangrene."

"Don't worry," Doctor Preece says, "you have the top medical attention available. Your hand could very well be almost good as new, with just a small loss in mobility."

Well, soon I'll know. In a few days they're going to do some tests, then final surgery.

~

"Mosquitoes sure are bad," I say.

We walk up the road that gleams in the full moon, our arms entwined. At Betty's we turn in through the windbreak.

"We can visit a while longer," says Betty.

"We'll be eaten alive," I say.

"Let's go in Dad's toolshed."

We angle across the moon-bathed clearing toward the shed. We close the door quickly behind us.

"Leave the light off," I suggest, "it'll attract less bugs."

"And less attention," Betty says.

The tools look mysterious, bathed in cool blue light. Betty's fingers follow mine, as if we're on the same journey, over the hammer, the rasp, the pliers, as my fingers drag along the jagged saw edge, Betty's travel its smooth band. I catch her hand as it reaches the handle, turn her. She props herself against the work-bench, I lean against her, our lips moving closer, nervously. They touch and we hold like this, holding still, our mouths unsure, our bodies pushing to get closer, closer, like we want to pass through each other's skin. My teeth press against my lips that press against hers. It hurts but it feels good. Her hands run up and down, clutching skin through my T-shirt. My fingers circle on her. Lips moving, wetter now. My hand slides, curves her breast, squeezes, slips to her waist, hip, her thigh, and I crouch to reach her knee, the edge of her loose skirt, pull the skirt up, my hand running up the inside of her leg to a soft... clank! I feel Betty go bolt straight. We're frozen in full light.

"Hm-ahm." A head pokes through the doorway. Betty's father. I stiffen. He steps in. His eyes are sharp darts stabbing my face. His gaze lowers. I follow his glance to Betty's skirt, caught high between our close hips. I step away. The skirt falls.

"Sorry, Mr. Robertson. We were…"

His hands hit my shoulders, push me square back against the shed wall, his fists on my chest, the two-by-four stud stabbing my back.

~

Jilly and Warren Hoover lead off the dance, the way newlyweds are supposed to. Everybody's here for the party. The barn looks better than it ever has, the floor clean. I ought to know, I scrubbed it, pinned mother's big white bows on the beams. Betty helped me hang them.

Mom said, "I want it to look especially nice since Jilly is the first one of you to tie the knot."

"The noose," I said.

When Jilly got engaged, Mom said to me, "Now that young Jilly's getting married, you'd better get thinking about a wife. You're twenty-four. I don't want to look after you forever." And she said it in front of Betty. Bad timing. I was damn mad. Now Mother's fussing over Jilly and Warren, kissing and hugging them, patting their backs. Fuckin' Jilly. Everybody with that weird rosy glow. Weddings make people mushy as porridge. Betty keeps looking at me with milky eyes. I don't feel mushy. No need to, now that Betty and I are engaged.

~

Wham. Jolt. Light burns right through my closed eyelids. Voices. Can't make out the words. Shadows bob. Shape of shoulders, heads. Can't open my eyes. I'm me, but somebody else. Shouts and rattling. Pressure. Jolt. In my chest. That chest. That body jolts again. Rests. Floating. Up. Toward the light.

~

"Don't come near my daughter or my property again, Delbert!" shouts Mr. Robertson, pushing me out the shed door.

When I get home, Mom's waiting for me.

"Stand here," she says pointing to the round rug in the kitchen. "Hold out your palms."

Whacks with the back of the wooden hair brush... Fourteen, whack! Fifteen, whack! Sixteen, whack!

"One for each year of your age. If you're smart you'll put these years behind you," Mother says, her voice trembling, angry. "You're too old to blame your evil on innocence. You're of an age to have sense and conscience, aren't you?"

"I guess so."

"Time we had a grown-up man here. I can't be everything. Start acting like someone with a future. You think about how you'll behave with girls from now on. Tell me about it tomorrow at breakfast."

My palms sting, hot and cold, blood red right near the surface of the skin.

"No dates until next summer. And keep away from Betty, or her father'll give you real cause for regret."

At breakfast my hands are swelled up and blistered so bad I can't use them. Can't even butter my toast. I eat it dry. Jilly and Ezz stare at me. Mom washes dishes. I feel her waiting. I feel her regret. I have nothing to say.

~

"I've got one more job to do, Betty, then we can have a dance or two," I say.

"Will it take long?"

"I have to deliver Jilly's change of clothes and a bouquet to their honeymoon suite."

"Can I come?" Betty asks.

"No, it's a secret where they're staying."

"I'm almost family."

"I said it's a secret. I'll be back."

Jilly and Warren are going to stay in the Hoovers' hired hands' cabin, because it isn't in use, and they can have privacy there. It's a short drive, about five miles, and once I'm there I poke around in the room just to imagine how they'll pass their honeymoon night. Looks like Mrs. Hoover's fixed it up with new curtains and bedspread. Crisp. Not too much to do, though, except go to bed, by the looks of it. I hang Jilly's outfit in the wardrobe, and put the flowers on the small table by the window. I lean on the bed to give it a test bounce. Firm, squeaks a bit. I pull down the sheets to see what they look like. Bright white and smelling clean and fresh. I take the small present out of my jacket pocket and place it in the centre of the bed. The sheet stains slightly at the edge of it as the handful of feathers float to rest in a halo around it. I tuck everything in, and head back to the party.

~

There aren't too many things I'd do differently except for that auger. If I could just go back, goddamn, I'd still have my hand where it ought to be. I keep replaying the scene in my mind, as it happened, and then as it should have happened. And I can almost believe that I have the power to go back and unclog the auger right. I mean, it wasn't even my fault. Betty asked if I'd disengaged the gears, but she doesn't know how men and machines work. It's the damn engineers. Should have designed some kind of safety catch on that blade. It would have saved me. Maybe I'll sue. But that won't click the clock back. Won't bring my life back to what it was. That's the only moment I want to relive. I'd keep my hand out of the auger. But you can't change things that are done.

~

"I'm back, Betty."

"You were gone a while."

"You missed me?"

"Can we dance now, Delbert?"

"In a minute. First I want to get a drink. Time to celebrate."

~

"I promise, Mom. I won't pluck any more live birds."

"Good to know you've learned a lesson. Now go and promise the same to Jilly and Ezz."

"No!"

"Yes! Do it."

"No! I won't!" I yell, turning to run out the kitchen door.

The best place to be is by myself in the bush. No one to attend to, no people watching me. When I'm sure I'm alone, I search around for stones the right size, load my slingshot, pull the pebble back with my left hand, squint past my thumb, hold my right hand bolt-steady, narrow the stone's path to a feathery target sitting on a branch. I can shoot them smack out of the air. I'm a deadly hunter.

BODYPRINTS

Benedict barely hears it. A swish. Like fabric, the rustle of leaves against his door. So soft and quick, he might have imagined it. It prompts him to get up from his desk, open the door to the twilighted woods. He breathes deeply, hunches his shoulders, shrugs to release the tension, leans his head back, exhales. When he turns to go inside, a shape catches his eye. Fish. There on the door: three fish. He blinks. Fish, suspended, as if they had swum through the forest, pressed up against his door, left their bodyprints, and swam on.

With a fingernail he scrapes at the fishprints, but they seem indelible, trapped in the plane of his door, out of their element. He glances back toward the woods, searching for some movement or person, an explanation. Nothing. He closes the door and returns to the desk, but his mind hovers with the fish. Distraction is easier than work and his hands feel stiff anyway. The keyboard has become a leaden accomplice to failure. He stares at his static fingers. He feels no spark, no freshness. He pushes his chair back from the desk, his hands reaching for the comfort of the tumbler on the side table.

After several shots of Irish whiskey, he slips into bed, picks up the book from the floor bedside him, flips it open, and plunges into Ingmar Bergman's autobiography. Bergman writes about Ibsen's masterbuilder, Halvard Solness, and his climb up the high tower he's built. A daring, foolhardy feat, spurred perhaps by receding potency, by the "astringent taste" of failure. Benedict imagines that taste, the whiskey thick on his tongue. Weary, he slips readily into sleep, into troubled dreams.

In the morning, Benedict rises with reluctance, but rises nonetheless. When he opens the cabin door, the fish are still there, but they have moved, have swum around in their confines to new positions. Or is he imagining? He inhales, trying to suck the clarity out of the morning air, then lugs his uninspired body up the path.

In the cafeteria, Benedict eats in silence amid the din. Bran in milk, and peach halves. He does not look up as a woman with short rust-coloured hair slips onto a chair across the table from him. Her red lips thin as she draws on a cigarette, and her eyes trail a slow exhalation of smoke toward the ceiling.

"I've been up all night again."

He looks up from his bran. Ashen circles under her eyes, dark piercing eyes in a skim-milk complexion.

"Hello, Amanda. Insomnia still got you?"

"It's a double bind. When I can't sleep at night, I can't paint in the day. So no time is productive. Do I look tired?" she asks.

"Tired. I'd say so. I'll get you a coffee."

"Black. Thanks."

Benedict steps around art portfolios and backpacks on the way to the urn, fills two cups with steaming coffee, palms a capsule of Creamo, juggles his way back to the table. To his surprise he finds Amanda's chair empty. *Gone*, he thinks, *good*. Amanda is a complicated business. *Too complicated*, he thinks. He sips his coffee, gazes, drifts between fact and speculation, then turns his attention to a newspaper, the *Globe and Mail*, left on the table.

Benedict walks the wooded path to his writing studio through the sheltering rows of spruce, a dark reach of forest impermeable to light, that whispers with wind. The branches at the bottom are brittle, bare. As the trees strive for height, they offer a flourish of needles and cones toward the sun. Up there birds perch and call. Crows, falcons, wrens. A whole unreachable world, a bright, exuberant world. Down below he steps in shadows, led by the narrow depression that marks the path. A spear of light jabs the woods where he breaks into the clearing and approaches his cabin. On the door, his fish swim. Benedict enters and moves directly to his desk. He is filled with an urgency to work. To be finished. To be rid of the anxiety that nags at him from the pages of his story outline. He pushes the old Remington aside, slides the small stack of paper in front of him, flips the pages open. He sharpens his pencil. Begins doodling in the margins around the paragraphs, sketching ideas for dialogue and direction.

Late in the afternoon, Benedict emerges from his studio. In a pool of sunlight, on the lowest step, sits Amanda, hunched close to the ground. Dressed in grey and cinnamon, melding with the dappled woods. She turns her eyes up to him.

"Hello," she says.

"What are you doing?" Benedict asks.

"I couldn't work."

Benedict turns out the inside light, closes the door.

"Why did you come here?"

"I guess I want to talk to someone." Amanda stands as he descends the porch steps.

"Maybe you're trying to function in the wrong realm. Why not paint at night and sleep days?"

"Then I'd miss things."

"Nothing important."

"But how would I know?"

They are silent, each waiting for the other to speak.

"I'm going to the cafe," he says.

"I'll go that way."

They walk through the spruce forest, the soft clud of their footsteps counterpointing the repeated chirp of a solo cricket.

"How'd you like my fish?"

"What fish?"

"On my cabin door."

"Didn't see them."

"Thought you might know how they got there."

"Beats me... Fish? In the woods?"

"Yeah, three."

"Dead?"

"Not dead, exactly."

"A photograph?"

"No, like fingerprints, but whole fish bodies."

"I don't get it."

A breeze soughs.

"I love the woods," he says, "the trees speak a mystical language."

"The noises make me nervous."

"Everything makes you nervous, Mandy."

"Thanks for your generous assurance," she says, "I feel so much better now."

"Sorry."

They break free of the trees, the shape of the central complex just ahead. Benedict angles toward the cafe.

Amanda follows, asks, "What are you going to do now?"

"Have a sandwich, think, read."

"Can I join you? Can we talk for a while?"

"Sorry. I have a producer on my neck."

"You had time for me before."

"Yes."

"I was convenient."

"Not exactly." Benedict reaches for the door handle at the entrance.

"Inconvenient, then."

Benedict hesitates. "We aren't in sync."

"We sink, or we swim," Amanda says.

Benedict raises his eyebrows, turns his left hand palm up, a gesture of resignation. Then he passes through the doorway and lets the door close, Amanda staring after him as his shape disappears into the hallway, leaving her own wan reflection in the glass.

Benedict bites into a grilled cheese sandwich. He relaxes, comforted by this ordinary, simple meal. He wonders how his grand masters, Ibsen and Bergman, found comfort, how they must have occasionally relished a baguette, a rusk with butter. He is certain that for them even the mundane glowed with a kind of greatness. But not so for himself. He watches the waitress. With few customers to serve, she busies herself wiping the counter and stacking plates. She's served him before in one or other of the dining areas. Beneath her efficiency, she has poise, a grace of movement. He prides himself on his powers of observation. *A writer's essential curiosity*, he thinks. Besides, she's pleasing to his eye. And the grilled cheese is good. Good indeed.

Back at his desk, Benedict scribbles a bit. His eyelids grow heavy, his head nods. He squints and shrugs to clear the cobwebs, takes another belt of Jamieson's, rattles his fingers over the keys, stops, crumples pages, and types some more. Since midnight, working, struggling through what feels like desertion by his art, desertion by language, by ideas, by his voice. No return in sight. His hand on the whiskey bottle.

Knock. Knock. Benedict lifts his drooping head from the page he's been blinking at, looks at the clock. Four a.m. Knock. Knock. Knock.

"Who is it?"

"Lucretia, who else?"

"Amanda. I'm working."

"I'm not."

"I gather that, but I plan to continue."

"Till when?"

"Till I'm done."

"Oh. All right."

He hears her footsteps on the stairs, the footfalls retreating into the forest. He stretches his arms above his head, tries to draw his concentration back. What there was of it is broken. He turns toward the crackling flame in the fireplace. Gazes at the dancing shapes, tilts forward on his chair. With a squeak it levels, and he pushes himself upright, stretches again. He crouches to poke the fire, steps back and watches the flames dance. When he opens the door and peers into the forest, the pitch black is probed by outpouring cabin light. The trees are restless, branches reaching in the wind. The air nips at his fingertips. The scents of darkness, crisp. A sweetness from the trees. An alkaline whiff, perhaps from the lake, out there beyond. An emptiness smelled only at night. And in the woods, wings ruffle above the swishing. A high-pitched screech. He feels edgy. He glances at his fish companions. He turns to go inside.

"Benedict," Amanda steps from the dark into the pool of light, "I'm cold." The accelerating wind agitates the trees. "I was waiting."

"For what?"

The clatter in the trees is a hundred pairs of hands rattling bones in cloth sacks.

"I'm cold."

"Do you want to come in, then, to warm up?"

Amanda grinds a cigarette into the soil under her boot.

"Yes. To get warm," she says.

Benedict closes the door behind them, returning the trees to darkness. Amanda moves to the window, her back to him. Her reflection in the pane is superimposed over the fretful dark, the firelight glinting in her hair. She sobs. He waits, then speaks.

"I don't know what to say."

Amanda's shoulders lift and fall, arms at her sides.

He tries again, "Did you see the fish?"

"I want you."

Benedict's lips thin to a wince.

"But you don't want me," she says, without turning.

Benedict is silent.

"Right?" she asks. She shivers, hugs herself.

"It's over, Mandy. We collided, it was an accident. We ricocheted apart. It's been over for months, over before it began really. I'm sorry."

Amanda turns, eyes wet with longing. Her arms reach around him in a tight clasp.

He pushes her arms. "No. Warm yourself by the fire."

"Hold me."

"I can't."

Amanda's shoulders slump.

"We're not at this place to stir up drama," Benedict says, "We're here to listen and to paint, to write. To be with our own selves."

"I came because you were going to be here."

"I came to work. Go to your studio and concentrate on the canvas. That's the best thing you can do, for both of us."

"Fuck off."

Benedict's joints feel like cardboard. Air sucked from the room. He moves toward the door, throws it open. A clattering presence dances on the porch, bites at the window, white pellets bounce crazily on the sill. Amanda doesn't move. He pushes the door partway closed, peers out. Ice bullets machine-gun the brittle air.

"Hail, big as marbles." He sticks his hand out to try and catch one. "Strange, coming at this time of night."

"I guess I'll have to wait it out," Amanda says, "if that's okay."

Benedict juggles two pellets in his palm.

"Never mind, I'll go." She bumps past him and disappears through the doorway. Hailstones bounce into the room at Benedict's feet.

"Amanda... " Benedict says through the open door, his voice drowned by the drumming ice.

Benedict wakes late, and sluggish. He lies in bed thinking, raises up on his elbow, and reaches for his pencil and notebook on the side table. He opens the book, writes.

Bergman? Loved leading ladies, but portrayed real wife in films. Yet brilliant.

Ibsen? Less courageous than the women he wrote.

Triumph over weaknesses. Created!!

Idly, he draws a circle. Writes *A* in it, then draws another, writes *B*. Tries to unload all the clutter that Amanda has brought into his mind. He doodles until his scratchings are small fish shapes. The pencil drops from his hand. Shadows on the ceiling move in the dawning light. *I'll simply imagine myself as Bergman*, he thinks. He gets up, slips on his jeans and sweater and moves directly to the desk. His fingers begin the rapid clacking of the typewriter keys.

Benedict shifts the phone receiver to his other ear. "Yes, Eldon. Still-life paintings... Let me try again. Each key scene starts as a tableau. I'll see the main guy and his lover Ingrid in scenes that make reference to classic symbolic icons... Yeah, Jungian, with painterly overtones... no, no, it's not that complex. Fax? Not yet, I'm still tuning... right, you want plot trajectory... scenes... Yes, I'm working on it. Hang with me, it's going slower than expected... A couple of days, Wednesday. I'll call you." Benedict hangs up the phone, points his finger at his head, thumb cocked, then lets the thumb fall. He closes his notebook, steps out of the booth.

There is no one in the cafeteria. At the counter, Benedict pours a coffee and chooses a chocolate-coated doughnut from the pastry basket, moves to the cashier.

"Hi," he says. "You served me at the cafe yesterday."

"Yes... grilled cheese," she replies, taking his money.

They laugh.

"You remember people by their meals?"

"Sometimes." She hands him his change. "Are you in one of the programs here?"

"I'm in the colony, writing... a screenplay, allegedly."

"How's it going?"

"Good, bad... I'm swimming upstream... oh god."

"What?"

"My life is full of fish," says Benedict.

"Pardon?"

"It's a long story. Fish in a forest. That about sums it up."

"I think I'm missing something."

"Three fish on my cabin door. You don't know if that's normal for cabin fourteen, do you?"

"I just collect money here. I don't know what weirdness goes on out where you *artistes* are."

"Hey, come on, I bet you're one of us when you're not wearing that apron."

"Well, I am in the extended theatre program," she says.

"Thought so."

"You've been speculating on me."

"I just watch people... for research."

"Then you put those people into your scripts?"

"If I'm lucky. The ideas don't always come together with the words."

"The words go swimming past you as if they were blue fish," the waitress says.

"Pardon?"

"Jack Spicer."

"The poet?"

"Yes, it's a Spicer line."

"Spicer's one of my favourites," Benedict says.

"Actors know all kinds of things."

"Say, did you put the fish on my door?"

"Are they blue?"

"No."

"Maybe they're a good omen. Imagine blue fish, and the words will come."

"I think they're a curse." Benedict shakes his coins in two hands.

A wave of exuberant voices enters the room, a rush of people to the lunch counter.

"Time to work," the waitress says, reaching for a stack of trays.

"Nice chatting. See you." Benedict pockets his coins, slips his notebook under his arm, and picks up his snack.

It's not words that are the problem, it's the right words. Benedict paces the small cabin floor. It's not sentences he wants, but magic.

Bang! The door flies open and Amanda bursts in. Takes a run at him, whirls away from his hands. Grabs the closest thing to her, a pile of pages on the desk, and pitches them into the fire. They begin to smoke, then flare.

Benedict freezes in disbelief, then leaps, jabs his hand into the flames, pulls out a smouldering clump, drops it to the tiles, stomps. He crouches to finger the pages. Black ash flakes in his hands. Amanda watches him. He stands up. Grasps her arms, half-turns her and shoves. She resists, leaning into him. He wrestles her out the door, slams and locks it. Amanda hammers with her fists on the outside.

Benedict drops into his chair, stares at the charred pile of papers. He leans his forehead into his hand. The banging stops. Silence gives way to the cracking of branches. Random bumps and crashes, stones and twigs thrown at his walls. Then nothing.

The glow in the fireplace burns down slowly. Benedict sits until it is reduced to smouldering embers. He rises, picks up the blackened pages of his script. Crouches before the hearth and blows on the coals. He holds one sheet in the embers till it catches fire, then hands in another sheet, another, until he sets the whole wad of paper into the blaze, lays a log on top.

Benedict pulls his chair snug to the desk, takes a pencil in his hand, picks up the small sharpener. Skin shavings peel away. The grinding grates his flesh, makes him feel its thinness. He angles the pencil towards his eyes, the lead a sharp, tiny spear point; the wood fresh, almost pink. He touches it to the paper, making a dark speck. And another that turns into a word. Then words, words that strain into sentences.

Benedict lifts his head, leans back, shrugs his shoulders, stiff from concentration. He pats the pages into a neat stack. It is pitch dark out the window. He is depleted, but eerily calm. His mind emptied into the hour of the morning when situations appear their most insoluble, deep-water black, fathomless black; or their most clear, agleam, crystal sharp with light. Depths in which Benedict sees direction, but not his destination.

He takes a blank piece of paper, scribbles some words and puts it on top of the pile of pages. He gets up and slips his arm through the strap of his backpack, hoists it onto his shoulder. The slight heft of his notebook, water bottle and binoculars makes a light load as he moves through the doorway into the darkness. So dark that he cannot see the fish, the steps, or even his hand reaching out in front of him to sweep away the branches as he walks through the forest, out of the woods.

The gravel road rides the top of a ridge. Benedict follows it about a mile, then he turns off and starts down into a coulee. A slight orange crack has opened in the sky. The slope is steep and he must descend sideways, planting his feet carefully on small bush-clumps, or in hollows in the sandy earth. Leaning his body in, hand ready to grab the scrubby sage or berry bushes. With just a few slips and scrambles he makes it to a small flat meadow filled with yellow wildflowers that appear iridescent in the faint pre-dawn light. The scent is sweet as he crosses toward the worn impression of an animal trail. He hears some kind of bird calling scratchily in the bush. Hunching, he moves into the path, a narrow way broken almost to shoulder height, about the height of an adult deer. He imagines himself as an animal for whom this bush is home. Its musky scent. Its mysterious warrens known intimately by feral beings, crouched, dart-eyed. He stops, his vision blocked by the gnarl of leaves and branches. He breaks ahead, as quietly as he can, a crashing clumsy intruder. The tangle of brush sends the path bending, pressing him low, almost to his knees, before it opens into a temple-like grove, where he stands among tall trees and looks straight up, turning slowly, a green spire circling above.

Benedict could turn back, but that is not why he came here. He presses on. The rustling near him sounds like his own. When he stops, the rustling, too, stops. When he resumes, it follows. The bird calls again, a deep croak. He recognizes the cry, but cannot place it. The underbrush thickens, the light ungenerous, though dawn is bright somewhere above. He pushes against the thick bush. A black viney branch snares his shoulder, thorns clutch his pant leg, jagged leaves graze his face. He heaves his weight forward. Throws himself at the knotted wall. Again, and again, until he is part of the tangle, his body held in the unyielding weave. He twists, trying to shift his pack, breathes deeply, his twisting tying him into the bush's grip. Tries to draw calm into his lungs, his body, his mind. The rustling brush beyond him is constant, and beyond this he hears the shushing of waves on the shore. Again the bird cries. This time he knows. A mist descends. With it a cooling. A shiver up his backbone. The flickering leaves swimming at his eyes.

His mouth opens. A call that gurgles at the base of his tongue. Breathing water.

"H-h-hhhhh..."

And with each breath, his body makes a tiny movement. A slight bend. A narrow arch. A shudder. Again, the heron calls.

Something in You Reaches

The shape walks away. Into a landscape of pencil lines, curves, erasures, occasional smudges of colour. Obviously human, though not fully composed. The hair grey. The coat filled in, beige from the shoulder down one side, the other side empty. An arm holding something without weight. Feet a blank that floats the torso above the ground. Behind the lines and forms, where paint is not laid in, the canvas fills with textured white. You study the figure. It appears to be a woman. Woman who walks away, toward the form she is becoming.

She will gain substance. An overcoat. An air of loneliness. A curved hand. Black shoes. An ache in the heart. She will become something in you that reaches toward her. Will reach as she walks away. And reach. A brush dabs at her, pokes her, strokes, slides around her. Lifts her out. Brings her to the ground.

When the painter paints, her attention splits, perhaps in three.

One. Intuitive movement. Dab. Step back. Tilt of head. Her brush blending. Giving shape.

Two. Idle attention to daily matters. Coffee schedule. The beloved. The garden that needs tending. An expected letter. A vague pain.

Three. Music that fills the air. By Albinoni. And she feels through the brush the woman walking. A dignified adagio. The place she walks bristles into being. The trimmed grass. And now framing her, protecting her, the thick trunks of stately elms. All this in the drifting habitation of thought and intuition. Brought into harmony by consideration, by the careful hand, the knowing eye. L'oeil savant. The pliant oil. Flows. Furls into desired space. Sensual. Turn of wrist, flex of fingers, the whole arm sweeping the space of desire.

You watch. You feel, as she paints, the transformation. Not only on the canvas. But in her. An emanating aura, not just of colour, but of energy, pouring through the gleaming eyes, the sure hand. A state of peaceful confluence. Describing this you wish for substance other than words. You imagine a still pond. A soft wind buffeting day lilies to a gentle sway. A complete presence in the sounding smelled thinking stroked lifting moment. The phrases you fall back on frustrate in their deficiency.

Growing there, in luminescent oil, by her right knee, fresh Swiss chard, rhubarb, carrot greens, and the slim baguette. From the eternal market, born into her sack, her burden of constant necessity. Borne to tables, bag after bag, the measure of her years. Out of paint comes freshness. Out of paint comes age. She walks on. Brushed by time. You follow.

Your eye careens across the grass, caresses the vaulting span that lies before her. The curve that reaches for the sky. For heaven. A note blooms out of silence, hovers, diminishes. The arching reach that lifts, holds, descends.

The painter squeezes tubes of raw colour. Mixes. Drops a brush into a jar of solvent. Considers the balance of background and fore-ground. The colours that compel. The tones that drop away.

The woman walking. Not walking. Her coat of paint. Her plain overcoat. This shroud. The bend of her legs in weariness. Drawn to the cathedral-arch. Bridge to another place. Vaulted arc. Defiant of gravity. Elevates the gaze beyond the magic key. Stone note at apex suspends the melody. Brush curling at the height. Flexing in the undercurve. Painting a trick of promise. A sleight of hand. Feint for the eye. Bridge that spans her whole horizon. Transports. The ecstatic possibility. The lure of radiant light. Hues of blue and sand. Transfigurative emanation.

The arches curve the woman. Are the curve of woman. Of earth. Of the bent hand that moulds. That cast you. You are drawn. You listen closely, the brush scruffs the surface, restless, laying down the oiled shade. In loving gaze. At breast. In the arms of. Serenity.

She walks. Weighted. Toward the elegant bridge. Your eye travels with her. And you see what she does not see. That the bridge deceives, though it appears to cross the river, ground to ground. And it is her ground that holds her. And the sublime curving span turns back.

Not a failed promise. This return that takes the eye where it has been. The loop, always back, but never in repetition. Never in defeat. She walks. You walk to become the one you have always been. You are painted this way. You are a shifting hue of your own colour.

White canvas stroked away. Dabbing at her pale clasping hand. Corner of sky swept in. Translucent cerulean. Wisp of cloud. Last whisper of the brush.

Stepping back. All of you stepping back. The painter, placing the wooden brush stalk to her lips, the woman, you. Back. Back from the painted plane.

In the painting's field. The arcing elm. The rustling grass. The river. Her black shoes. The bridge's flight. Movement. Becoming. The daily bread.

WEIGHTS & MEASURES

B-L-U-E M-O-O-N. The big letters hang, lit by a sickly yellow light, on the side of the hulking building. The real moon, a translucent crescent, sits high and elegant above. To Lily it seems as if a strand of light stretches, connecting the sign and the tip of the moon. She blinks, and the filament thins but remains.

A few vehicles dot the parking lot on this dark edge of town. As Jeff slows the car and turns off the highway toward the building, a car in the middle of the lot accelerates and fishtails, spraying gravel through a ninety-degree arc. The car, a Camaro, straightens out and zips by in a cloud of dust.

"Are we sure we want to go in there?" asks Lily.

"This was your goddamn idea. 'It's just a little further,' you said, 'Just a little further.' We've been going a little further for two and a half hours. I'm not going another inch without some food."

Jeff wheels the car between two pick-up trucks, shuts it off. He and Lily step into the warm night. Jeff slams his door, stuffs his hands in his jacket pockets, walks ahead of Lily toward the entrance.

"Rick's directions were bad. I'm sorry," says Lily to Jeff's hunched shoulders. The crunch of gravel underfoot is his only reply.

The door closes behind, and they enter a foyer, eerie in gaudy shades of orange-purple-red lit by pinball and shooting games that line the walls. One lone figure, lost in concentration, perches on a tall stool, pushes the flipper buttons on Cosmic Comet. Jeff and Lily pass through the wash of garish light.

Lily raises her hand to eye level, "Look at the colour. I have alien skin," she says. Jeff glances then looks away.

They enter a cavern of a room. On the left is a long sit-down bar with a dark wood railing, and a ripple of light and shadow from fabric-covered, low-hanging lamps along its length; on the right, beyond a glittering bank of gold-coloured potted plants, shines a large empty dance floor; straight ahead at the far end, set off by a spindled wooden railing, is a brighter area with an expanse of dining tables, where a waitress is setting knives and forks and napkins.

Jeff leads the way toward the dining room, angles to a table in the corner at the edge of the dance hall and separated from it by a low wrought iron rail. Before they're settled, a waitress approaches, steaming pot in hand.

"Evening. I'm Verna. Coffee?"

Lily smiles, pushes her cup forward, studying the woman's black uniform, white apron, white collar, and the black and white cap held in place by two bobby pins. Jeff watches the movement of her hands as she pours coffee into his cup, her fingernails blood red.

"Menus?"

"Please," answers Lily.

Verna sets the menus down and moves away. Lily and Jeff sip coffee, ponder the selections, and glance up, taking in their surroundings. This dinner club has a faded glitter, the dog-eared feeling of a place that once pulsed with lively bodies and zesty energy. Now it's a heel too worn down to repair, a carpet stain permanent with age.

Jeff speaks distractedly, not toward Lily, but out into the room. "There's hardly anyone in here... could hold three hundred."

"It's suspended in another time," says Lily as Verna returns to their table to take their orders.

"Steak sandwich, rare, and onion rings," says Jeff.

Lily pauses for one last consideration, then orders, "House salad, please, Italian dressing."

"That'll be about seven, eight minutes," Verna says, turning on her heel toward the kitchen.

An electronic squeal cuts through the air. A voice, tinny but enthusiastic, rattles down from high in the rafters. "Two minutes to showtime." As the syllables echo and fade, a man in a powder-blue dinner jacket ambles across the empty dance floor toward the bandstand. He moves without zeal, carries a glass of beer in his right hand. He is Chet, the band leader. Portly, shoulders sloping forward in the resigned slump of a man whose hopes have not been answered. He wears a small dark peaked cap, snug over his long, straggly, ash-coloured hair. He pauses at the edge of the bandstand, glances behind him. He climbs the steps, reaches for his guitar.

From the direction of the bar, another blue-jacketed figure moves onto the shiny floor. Kenny struts with an air of cool confidence, once an affectation, now a natural gait. He jabs out his cigarette as he passes a round-topped table with an ashtray at its edge. He steps onto the stage, grabs the neck of his Fender bass, swings the strap over his shoulder, clips it on, flicks his amp switch, thumbs the bottom string, sending out a low resonant tone. Chet picks a few notes on his guitar. They tune together.

From the farthest corner a third man in pale blue hustles into the dance hall, a youthful spring in his step. He crosses the floor, jumps onto the stage and moves deftly between microphone stands and amplifiers, slips in behind the drum set. The bass drum thumps once as Bobby fits his foot to the pedal. Chet steps to the mike.

"Thangyou. Now-the-second-set-at-the-Blue-Moon. For-your-dancin'-pleasure-John-Fogerty's-'Proud-Mary.'" A drum beat snaps on cue, and a lounge-band interpretation, mellow but punchy, fills the empty hall, the dining area, the bar.

Lily's body is angled in her chair; her eyes look away from Jeff, toward the band. He watches her. As if she can feel his stare, Lily turns.

"You're still bugged," she says.

"Not really."

"Sure you are."

"Okay, so I'm bugged." Jeff shifts his eyes from her face, turns his head away. Lily stares at his profile. A tear wells in the corner of her eye. She turns her gaze back toward the stage. The music feels distant to her, but her toe begins tapping to the beat.

Chet moves automatically through the familiar melody. He can play and sing these tunes in his sleep. He loves music, but the relentless drudgery of miles in the van and twenty years of sitting on vinyl chairs in grimy bars is a grinding gear in him. The road he feels most alive on is the one he rides on his Harley when he gets back home. On his hog, astride its muscle, he rides to clear his circuits, air rushing in his ears, a rumble between his legs. In his black leathers and with flat-out power he out-races gloom.

Kenny has his looks. There is never a crack in his poise, a stumble in his walk, a hair out of place. His veneer is polished smooth. Life on the road, though wearing, is bearable, because there are always women to engage with his charm. His music too is slick, buffed up by years of playing. He and Chet have picked and sung their way around the country for a decade. Their harmonies and counterpoints fit, easy and familiar, programmed by endless repetitions.

Young Bobby, Bobby-boy, they call him, is a hot drummer.

He's new but he knows where he's going. He's paying his dues, refining his licks night after night with his sticks in his hands. He plays every style, and sings with feeling. Soon he'll be off to New York, or Toronto, or Nashville. He'll soon be where the action is, where the breaks are, laying down the backbeat in the spotlight of fame.

No one dances.

"They're pretty good," Jeff says.

Lost in her own thoughts, Lily offers no response, so he shifts his attention back to the band.

As if in slow motion, Lily turns toward him, "They look quite worn out, underneath the snazzy jackets."

"What'd you expect? Bar to bar. It's a hard life," says Jeff.

"Everybody's life is hard sometimes."

"But not... oh, forget it."

As the song ends, Verna arrives with the dinner plates balanced on her right hand and forearm, side dishes in the other hand. She sets the plates in front of each of them.

The familiar Creedence Clearwater beat continues, and a chorus of "Lodi" counterpoints the click and plink of plates and cutlery.

"Enjoy," says Verna, and turns away.

Jeff sprinkles HP sauce on his plate, dips the corner of the sandwich and takes a bite. Lily forks a cucumber to her mouth.

After a while Lily pauses. "How's your steak?"

"Fine."

"Feels better with a bit of food in your stomach, doesn't it?"

"I'm all right," says Jeff.

"But you're not really, are you?"

"If you already know, why ask? Lay off, I just want to eat."

Jeff stuffs two onion rings into his mouth. He waves his coffee cup in the direction of the waitress. Lily's gaze lifts from her salad to the turning mirror-ball above the dance floor, its facets tossing shards of light, sparks flaring in the cavernous maw.

The guitar twangs the song's last riff.

"Thangyouverrmuch. Fogerty-times-two." Chet's patter, reduced to formula and minimum, is a brief break in the tempo, allowing a moment for tuning and repositioning. He turns his head quickly, looking down at the guitar neck, at the location of the fret, hits the first chord, jerks his head up, mouth to microphone. "And-now-a-classic-Hank-Williams-tune-'Cold-Cold-Heart.'" His long single earring flips against his cheek. The earring shows, at the same time, that he belongs, that he's different. He's been a gang member in Salt Lake City almost as long as he can recall. It's tough to keep in touch with the guys during tour gigs, but they always welcome him home. The fellas, the bikes, the partying, that's what he likes; not the fights, cops and jails, the chicken. Chicken, chicks, chickie-flesh, women, he's had the trouble and lost the taste. Prefers it alone, him and his Harley, flying, escaping the weight, like a bird, like a bullet.

Kenny rocks back and forth, lays down the bass line, bobs his head, his salt and pepper hair. Right with it, but in control, smooth. Playing the bottom line, adding the dollars, planning the moves on the young waitress, worrying that she'll notice his thickening girth. He'll buy her a drink with his pay. The bucks. The dollars that keep him on the circuit. The dollars he sends to his ex-wife and his kids, Kenny Junior and little Julie. Kids who would be proud, he's sure, if they could see him play, kids who would love him, if only. And the wife, the life he left behind for the circuit where loneliness and need, games and opportunities, let him lead woman after woman into dingy hotel rooms. Always a fresh pair of eyes looking up, new breasts and hips to bear down on, to soften the edge. Kenny the performer, the promise, pressing, pushing in, pushing on.

Bobby, young Bobby, writhing to the rhythm, lashing out, crashing the cymbals, rattling the snare, thumping the bass drum, slashing the air with rapid-fire sticks. Bobby ablaze with music, igniting this band tonight. Bobby-boy with a girl in Boise, and a '56 Chev, and a drunk dad at home in Sudbury. Mom dead now two years, from nothing to live for. But Bobby has music, drinks milk, drives the band, keeps these old guys going. And you can't ignore a drummer, a drummer on the move. Hands carrying the downbeat in the night, into tomorrow. Pure heat. Fast-fingered and piston-kneed. Pounding his heart out. Smashing the skins to be heard in 'Frisco, in Paris, in Sudbury, in Boise. Wondering if she'll wait through the uncertainty, the distance. Does she hear his urgent rhythms? His heartbeat for her? Is she true? Will she wait? With a flourish he ends the song.

No one claps.

"Thangyouverrmuchpreeshyetit."

Jeff wipes the corner of his mouth with his napkin. Lily says, "They don't even look at each other when they play. Like a sad marriage."

"It's not a marriage. It's music. They don't need to look at each other," says Jeff, "they relate through the music."

"Like the music has replaced the person. Seems sad."

Chet's voice punctuates, echoing through the hall.

"And–now–back–to–back–rockers–from–way–back–the–brothers Everly–'Wake–Up–Little–Susie' and Buddy–Holly's–'Rave–On.'"

"What are you afraid of, Jeff?"

"Nothing."

"You afraid of me?"

Jeff drums his fingers on the table in time to the music. Looks into the space beyond Lily's head.

Lily continues, "So this is our getaway good time?"

"I guess so."

"Great. We're having such fun."

She looks at him. He glances down at the checkered table cloth. Her eyes are probes. He closes his eyes and takes a long slow breath. He thinks of being with her in the dark. How that's easier. There he can be blind, unseen, untouchable in places. Here in the light he removes himself, sits inside.

Lily pushes away from the table, rises, and walks purposefully to the centre of the dance floor. She begins to twirl and sway, and there's a "Yip" from the bandstand, spliced between beats and words. Lily bops in a freeform, dream-eyed, internal way. To the beat. Up and down. On sprung feet. Side to side. Shrug, turn, kneebend, arms out, slump, whirl. A style that defies interpretation. Spurred by the zest of music. And the band members smile, nod to each other. Occasionally in her spins she glimpses Jeff, seemingly glued to his chair.

A few patrons have moved closer to the dance floor. Verna leans on the kitchen pass-through, bobbing her capped head, clapping her hand on her thigh.

Lily bobs, her hair bouncing and flipping across her face. She kicks out her feet, bends and twirls.

"Rave on!" the band shouts. Cymbals crash the finale.

Lily swirls an imperfect pirouette, stops, bows her head, then applauds, laughing, and the band members clap back to her.

"Thangyouverrmuchthangyou."

"Thank you guys," says Lily, waving as she turns and moves off.

Jeff watches, his hands flat on the table, his eyes inexpressive. Lily stands in front of him, gulping water from her glass. The band begins a waltz-tempo version of "Blue Moon," their set-ender.

"That was some show," says Jeff.

"Glad you liked it. It wasn't for show. It was fun. They're okay. You're right. They're just making music. Let's go have a beer with them when they're done."

"No thanks."

Lily wipes her brow and takes another swallow. "I need some air."

The band moves into the chorus of the song. Lily's gaze holds on Jeff's face, waiting to meet his eyes. When he looks at her, she turns, walks out of the dining area, by the bar, and into the arcade.

Jeff remains seated, watches her until she disappears.

"Blue moon, you saw me standing alone..." sings Chet.

Jeff rises slowly, drops some money on the table. He walks through the big space, feeling conspicuous. Just before the exit, he pauses to look back. His gaze pans this place that clings stubbornly to its past. Verna, her back to him, is already clearing their table.

The band members, their set done, step down from the stage. Chet angles across the dance floor toward the pinball games, reaching into his pocket for quarters. Kenny struts toward the waitress who's leaning on the bar and without breaking stride he strikes a match and lights a cigarette. Bobby wipes his brow with a small towel. He looks around for the dancer and her companion as he makes his way to the back door to breathe Montana air, and to try and see as far away as Nashville.

Jeff turns and passes through the door. He stumbles slightly on the step, his shoes scuffling the gravel as he gains his footing. Looking up, he can't see Lily by the car, or anywhere in the parking lot. He wonders where she is.

"Lily," he calls.

He blinks, and again his eyes scan the light and the shadowy places, seeking her familiar shape.

THE WINDOW

The large second-storey window is set in a cream-coloured brick wall. It is visible from the alleyway that passes by the back yard. Or from the houses opposite, whose yards also face the alley. The window is approximately seven feet high by four feet wide. It reaches almost from the floor to the ceiling of the room it reveals to anyone who might be looking. A white blind is visible, positioned always at one of two extremes. All the way up during the day. Three-quarters down at night. It is now all the way up. Light falls through the window into the room, drawing the gaze.

A figure moves within the room, entering the pool of light occasionally, passing near the window from time to time. As it moves from the shadows into the light, it is possible to surmise that the person is a man. Something about the posture and shape of the clothing. Now the figure stops. His hair appears to be ash brown and he is wearing blue jeans and a green sweater. He stands looking down toward the lane. He props his right elbow on the window frame, leans his head against his extended right hand. He remains there, stationary, staring.

A slight reflection on the window casts a transparent image of the building on the other side of the lane. The one opposite that would allow a direct gaze into the room. This reflection, of course, is invisible to him.

He turns. Something in the room has demanded his attention. He moves away from the window, disappears beyond the frame's edge. It is now possible to see a dresser in the room on the wall directly opposite the window. A square mirror hangs over the dresser and reflects some of the light entering the room, reflects back the image of the window. A pink scarf is draped over the corner of the mirror. Shadows hover at the edges of the window-pool of light.

He re-enters from the left side, pauses, and looks over his shoulder toward an unseen part of the room. He seems to be watching, or listening. After a short time, he turns his head and moves forward in his original direction, disappearing beyond the right frame of the window.

Shadows of leaves dapple the brick wall and the surface of the window, a skin of fluttering lace.

From the right he passes into the field of the window. He stands full profile, facing left. The movement of his lips and jaw indicate that he is speaking. He abruptly turns, moves and disappears again at the right edge.

Stillness settles in the room, or at least in the part of the room revealed in the window frame. Attention shifts back to the flutter of light and shadow on the glass.

The figure passes... No, this is another figure. The emergence of this figure is unexpected, passing from the left to right sides, as if following him. The manifestation is too sudden and the movement too quick to reveal details about this person's identity. Yet, an indefinable impression lingers that this is a woman. But no further evidence materializes in the window. No one comes or goes.

Perhaps the action in the room has been concluded, the figures having moved to a room on another floor. Or maybe they have departed entirely from the house by a door that is not visible from this vantage. Perhaps they are lovers, caught in the room's corner now by raw passion, her leaning forward over a chair, him behind with his hands around her waist. Or maybe they are siblings visiting an aging aunt who wears a rose-coloured shawl, sipping tea in the living room. Or perhaps the second figure was the same person as the first, but in different attire.

Sun through waving leaves and branches continues to dab and sparkle on the glass. Nothing more is visible behind the pane. Careful observation reveal a subtle change in the reflections. The sun is shifting to an oblique angle, creating a creeping opaque glare on the surface of the upper part of the glass that begins to obscure the view into the room.

Movement. Discernible because it is close to the window. An arm reaches in from the right side, dropping an object that looks like a hat on what may be assumed to be a bed, perhaps a futon on a low platform, positioned just under the window. This surmise can be made since the crown of the hat is barely visible above the edge of the sill. The arm disappears, then returns in the bottom right corner. The line it forms cuts the corner of the window diagonally at an angle of about forty degrees. It seems the hand is resting on something— perhaps the bed— and is supporting a body that can't be seen, but that must be sitting on the bed. A shoulder moves scarcely in and out of view. The arm seems to belong to the woman.

He appears now from the right side. He stops dead centre and turns quickly. He is speaking. His gestures are large, his action intense. His words seems heated.

The arm moves. The figure straightens, shifting from the lower right to fill the corner of the low part of the window opposite him. The figure remains seated. The light from the window and the scrutiny allowed by the figure's stasis reveals long dark hair. This, and the quality of a gesture with the left hand, verify that this is a woman. She too is speaking in an animated fashion. No sound can be heard, but they seem to be speaking loudly and at the same time.

He turns away from her. Disappears to the left. She continues what is likely shouting, pointing her finger after him. The energy of her expression seems to indicate that he has left the room and she is shouting to be heard at a distance, or over some other noise. A shower, perhaps. A radio. A hair dryer.

The glare has disappeared, has given way to light filtered through clouds, and the wall and window have taken on a tawny, clay-like tinge in the grey light.

She rises. Lifts a packet from the window sill, a pack of cigarettes. She removes one, placing it between her lips, bright red with lipstick. Though the cigarette is a small object, it is quite distinctive, a bright white stalk against grey tones. She flicks a lighter in her left hand, moving the flame to the cigarette, her face flush to the pane. The light of the flame intensifies the red of her lips. She sets the pack and lighter back down on the sill. She pulls at the sleeve of the sweater, tweed with a taupe cast, that is draped over her shoulder, tucks it closer around her neck. She is young, perhaps thirty. She tilts her chin up and exhales a cloud of blue-white smoke into the air.

The odd ripple can now be seen splashing on the window. It has begun to rain.

Her ability to get close to the window indicates that the bed may not occupy the entire space beneath the sill. The bed must end just about where the hat is resting, toward the right. The floor must therefore be free by the left side, provided there are no pieces of furniture or piles of books. This seems to be the case. She continues smoking. A steady wisp drifts upward, above her head, and disappears behind the white blind.

Above the blind, at the top, a subtle arc graces the window frame. A single row of vertically-placed bricks features a slightly radiant pattern which creates this arc. This curve breaks the otherwise rigid angular patterns formed by the horizontal rows of bricks and the straight lines of the other three sides of the window.

He re-enters the frame, just visible behind her and over her left shoulder. He kneels on the bed and walks on his knees toward the window. She turns her head in his direction. This shift of her head reveals a strongly profiled nose. She looks down toward him. He is wearing a wine-coloured garment. The overlapping vee at the neck suggests a bathrobe, possibly velour.

The rain continues to splash on the window, the drops growing bigger in an increasingly vigorous downpour. The ripples, formed by descending streaks of water on the window, and the volume of water falling over the lane, distort his image and hers, making them appear amphibian.

Through the ripples it seems that he has resumed talking. He gestures with his right hand in an agitated manner. She begins speaking in response. The movement of their mouths and heads indicates that they are again shouting. Her left hand arcs out of the shadows toward his face. The blow knocks him against the window. His left shoulder collides with the glass. Raindrops jiggle, sparkling like tinsel, as the window shakes. He bounces up and leaps toward her, his hands reaching for her face. She dodges, moves back into the room. Her silhouette is visible against the mirror above the dresser. It is possible to see that her left arm is raised. He stands to the left, his back toward the window. She emerges once again into the light. In her left hand is the pink scarf. She lunges toward him, flips the scarf over his head, yanks him sideways onto the bed. Their bodies disappear, beyond the right side of the frame. Only their legs are visible, from below the knees to their feet. His legs kick underneath her. Gradually the kicking subsides, their legs entwined, unmoving.

It is growing darker. The metallic evening light flattens the colour of the brick to an ashen shade, a pewter sheen on the plane of the window. The glass slowly blackens as less light enters the room, and as no light inside is activated. It is impossible to distinguish any shapes in the room. The mirror is no longer visible. There seems to be no one there.

The rain diminishes, then ceases altogether. The ripples of water begin to dry on the glass, spotting it with dusty blemishes. The mortar lines demarking the bricks have disappeared in the waning light.

From the shadows of the room, a hand emerges, itself a shadow, pale, fluttering. It clutches the drawstring, pulls the white blind to a position three-quarters down, leaving just the bottom portion of the window a black solid. In night's descending darkness, the stark white of the blind stands out against the charcoal expanse of the wall.

There is time now to contemplate what has happened. A minor disagreement? A murder? What evidence prompts such conclusions? Perhaps the people were not angry, but joyous. Maybe they were lovers feigning conflict. Or perhaps the struggle was real, but after the blind was drawn, they made up, hugging and laughing. Or is there now a body in the room?

What should you do?

But for the blind, the wall becomes as dark as the sky, such that it seems to be swallowed by the night.

Are you certain of what you have seen?

A movement of the blind. The moonlight, playing on the glass. Perhaps you should watch the window a while longer.

End Notes

Acknowledgements and Permissions:

Epigraph from: Ludwig Wittgenstein, *Tractatus Logico-Philosophicus*, 5.634. Translated by C.K. Ogden. Routledge & Kegan Paul Ltd., in assocation with Methuen Inc.

"The words go swimming past you as if they were blue fish." (In "Bodyprints"): Jack Spicer. Excerpted from *The Collected Books of Jack Spicer*, copyright 1975 by the Estate of Jack Spicer, and reprinted with the permission of Black Sparrow Press. Line quoted appears in *The Heads of the Town, a Textbook of Poetry, 21*. Pg. 179.

Fictions from this collection have been published as follows:

"The Leak," in *Broadway Magazine*, Saskatoon. 1994.

"Hammond at the Bluenote," (different title), in *Rampike*, V.7, #2. Toronto. 1991.

"tie-burner," in *Grain. Vol. XVIII, #3*. Saskatoon. Fall 1990.

"Weights and Measures," in *Transition*, Spring/Summer Issue, Regina, 1990.

"painter," in *Ice River*, V.1, #2. Union, Oregon. 1987. And anthologized in *Sky High: Stories from Saskatchewan*, Coteau Books, Regina, 1988.